A MERRY MURDER ON RUFF ROAD

WAGGING TAIL COZY MYSTERY SERIES

CINDY BELL

CONTENTS

ISBN: 9781710739138

"*E*asy boys." Nikki Green pulled back just enough on the leashes of the two German Shepherds to create space between them and Princess. She knew the two larger dogs meant no harm, but Princess' yelp and crouched stance indicated she didn't know that yet.

"Who are these handsome fellows?" Sonia Whitter crouched down beside Princess and held out her hand to the two dogs.

"Rocky and Bruno." Nikki laughed as she rolled her eyes. "Cute names, right?"

"Absolutely." Sonia laughed as she gave them each a pet. "I didn't know you were taking on any new dogs. They are German Shepherds, aren't they?"

"I didn't either. Yes, they are German Shepherds, the same as Coco. I stopped by the animal shelter this morning to help out with breakfast and walks, and these two were there with Petra. A friend of hers was pet sitting them and he has broken his leg. He is going to need surgery, so Petra has them at her house and she asked if I could help out by walking them." Nikki winked at the two dogs that panted happily. "Of course, I agreed. The dogs ran right over to me."

"Of course they did. You're such a loving person, a dog person, they can sense that." Sonia met her eyes and smiled. "Nikki, I admire how you keep growing your business, and now you're helping Petra more at the animal shelter. Don't you think you're taking on a little too much, though?" She grinned as Princess took a few steps towards the bigger dogs, then let out a sharp bark. "Oh, someone wants to let them know who is in charge."

"Oh, they'll figure it out soon enough." Nikki laughed as she looked between the three dogs. She glanced up at Sonia and shrugged. "I'm happy to help out Petra, she does so much. Besides, I love being with the dogs and it's good for me to stay busy. Especially at this time of year. Growing up in Dahlia, Christmas was always a special time. But since my family has all moved away, it's just not the same."

"I know what you mean." Sonia sighed. "I've decided to stay close to home this year. But I am planning a holiday party at the Dahlia Hotel. I'm going to drum up donations for some local charities, and of course the shelter. I'm going over tomorrow to do a menu tasting and give final approval for the meal. I would love it if you would join me."

"Thank you, I'll be there." Nikki took Princess' leash from Sonia and added it to the two she already held. "I just really wanted to help Petra leading up to the holidays. After how hard she's been working, I know she needs it. Plus, I love getting to see all the puppies and kitties she has at the shelter. There are quite a few new rescues that have come in."

"Well, it sounds very busy this year." Sonia gave the German Shepherds another pat. "It's nice to meet you, Rocky and Bruno. I'm sure you will fit in just fine."

"I'm going to pick up Spots." Nikki smiled. Spots was a beautiful Dalmatian that Nikki's boyfriend, Quinn Grant, had recently adopted.

"How is Spots doing?"

"Great. But it has been an adjustment for Quinn." Nikki grinned. "Spots gets him up pretty early to go out, and his plan to keep Spots on the floor on his pillow, and out of his bed, has not worked out. Spots also snores."

"Poor Quinn." Sonia laughed.

"We should get going, I have a few errands to run after the walk." Nikki smiled. "I have to stop at the pet store to pick up some Christmas presents for the dogs. I need to make sure I don't leave it till the last minute. I don't want to end up with nothing to give out to the dogs for Christmas." She lowered her voice and grinned. "The rawhide chews I gave out last year were not a hit. I had a few complaints about the mess the dogs made with them."

"Oh, I bet." Sonia laughed and clapped her hands together. "Princess had hers scattered all over the house for weeks."

"Oops." Nikki grinned, then hurried the dogs down the driveway. Sonia was right about one thing, she did have a tight schedule, and if she didn't stick to it, she would never get everything done.

As Nikki walked briskly in the direction of Quinn's house to pick up Spots, she noticed the array of decorations that adorned the lampposts and fences throughout Dahlia. She loved how much effort everyone made to celebrate the holidays in the town. Each red bow, each string of tinsel wrapped around twinkling lights, brought up memories of her childhood in Dahlia. She smiled to herself as she recalled the empty lot being turned into a skating rink. The sharp sound of the ice skate blades cutting against the ice still sent a shiver along her spine.

Even after her brother started traveling across the country, working along the way, and her parents had moved away from Dahlia, she stayed, mostly because she couldn't imagine anywhere else being home. Her small apartment was just enough space for her. Her assortment of clients kept her financially afloat, and her love for their dogs fulfilled her. There wasn't much about her life in Dahlia that she didn't love, and since Quinn had become such a big part of it, she hadn't ever been happier. It still surprised her at times that she had ended up reunited with her high school crush, and that he had fallen as hard for her, as she had for him.

Despite her rush to get everything done, her heart warmed as she acknowledged just how lucky she was.

Once Nikki had collected Spots, and Coco, she steered the dogs towards the park. Many of her usual dogs were off on vacation with their owners. The small pack she walked made it easy for her to integrate the new dogs. Spots and Coco gave each of the dogs a sniff, then seemed more interested in the grass they strolled through. Nikki was pleased that Sonia had become more relaxed and let her beloved Chihuahua walk with the larger dogs. Nikki did take Princess on a few extra solo walks and Sonia would often join them. After their walk through the park, Nikki dropped off Coco and Spots, then checked her phone. There were no messages and she could spare a few minutes, so she decided instead of taking the dogs straight back home, she would walk through the shopping area to see more of the Christmas decorations.

"All right, we're taking a little detour." Nikki walked towards the center of town.

She relaxed as she walked down Ruff Road, the main shopping strip in Dahlia. The street teemed with cars and pedestrians despite the early hour and the cool temperature. Holiday shopping was in full swing. Nikki smiled and waved to a few of the people she knew. There weren't many that she didn't. She eyed a collection of people gathered around the window of one of the clothing shops. The front window displayed a wintry scene, including snowmen, gingerbread houses, and reindeer. The sight of the picturesque display immediately put her in the festive spirit.

As Nikki walked past Marlo's Butcher Shoppe, she was reminded that she wanted to pick up some bones that she'd ordered for Spots. He loved the raw bones and she loved treating him. The pup held a special place in Nikki's heart, and her heart warmed whenever she thought of how Quinn had recently adopted him. He had quickly stolen both of their hearts and become a part of Quinn's family. Although Spots was technically Quinn's dog, she often thought of him as hers as well.

Nikki looked at the dogs happily sniffing each other. They certainly seemed to be getting along.

"Good boys and girl." Nikki crouched down and gave each dog a pet. As she began to stand up, she heard the door to Marlo's shop open. She turned towards it and saw a man who she recognized as Scott, the delivery driver for Marlo's shop, come running out of the shop and straight towards her. She tried to step out of the way, but before she could he barreled into her. He knocked her off her feet and she landed hard on the ground with a thud.

"Stop him!" A tall, slender man she recognized as Gavin, a cook at the local diner, came running out of Marlo's shop and straight past her towards Scott. "Stop!" He shouted as he ran after him. "Stop right there!"

Nikki was in a daze as she got to her feet. Scott continued running. Followed by Gavin close behind.

"Get back here!" Gavin gasped for air as he attempted to shout.

The collision had knocked the wind out of Nikki. She wasn't sure what to do but the decision was made for her when the dogs tugged at the end of their leashes and started running towards Scott and Gavin.

The faster the dogs ran, the faster Nikki ran. She had no choice but to continue to run after the two men, as the two German Shepherds led the way. But it wasn't enough for Rocky. He gave a hard, sudden lunge and his leash broke free of her grasp. As soon as he sensed the freedom, he snarled and launched himself forward, running past Gavin with ease and quickly covering the distance between himself and Scott.

"No Rocky! Sit!" Nikki gasped as she chased after the dog.

Before Nikki could reach him, Rocky jumped up into the air and landed hard against Scott's back.

Scott stumbled and fell down onto the grass beside the sidewalk. Rocky stood on top of him. Bruno barked and whimpered as he attempted to break free as well.

"Stop! Please!" Scott squirmed on the ground but stopped moving when a loud growl emerged from Rocky.

"You killed him!" Gavin pointed at Scott. "You killed Marlo!"

CHAPTER 2

"What? Marlo's dead?" Nikki stared at Gavin.

"Not just dead. He's been stabbed. He's been murdered." Gavin put his hands on his hips and bent over as he tried to catch his breath.

Nikki's mind swam with the revelation. Had Scott really killed Marlo?

Why else would he run? Had people complained about him? She had heard that he was occasionally late for deliveries. Had Marlo fired him? Had they gotten into some kind of scuffle? She had no idea what the driver's motive was, but it appeared as if he was involved.

Nikki was snapped back to reality as Rocky growled while he restrained Scott.

In the distance, Nikki heard sirens headed in their direction. Someone had heard or seen the commotion, but she guessed they had no idea what had really occurred. They didn't know that the peaceful town of Dahlia, covered in cheerful holiday decorations, was about to be overshadowed by a murder.

"What did you do to Marlo, Scott?" Gavin glared at him. His entire body shook as he struggled to catch his breath. "Why did you kill him?"

"I didn't kill him. I swear. I didn't do anything." Scott shook his head as Rocky tugged hard at his sleeve and snarled. "Get him off me."

"Marlo has been murdered!" Gavin pointed at Scott. "He killed him!"

"I didn't!" Scott shouted. Rocky growled and continued to restrain him, while Bruno strained against the leash.

The two German Shepherds didn't appear to want to hurt Scott. Nikki, who had worked with all kinds of dogs as a dog walker, believed that they just reacted because of the commotion and wanted to stop him because he had knocked her off her feet and then run. Her heartbeat quickened as she edged towards Rocky.

"It will be okay. They just don't want you to

move." Nikki carefully picked up Rocky's leash and held it tight. She frowned as she wondered how to approach Rocky while still restraining Bruno. She didn't know much about the dogs, and it appeared as if they were not the best-behaved canines. If she did anything to pull Rocky free, Scott might escape. They weren't hurting Scott and she didn't want him to escape.

Nikki guessed that the dogs had strong protective instincts, though they certainly needed training.

"Rocky, calm down, boy." Nikki reached her hand towards him.

Rocky kept his teeth dug deep into Scott's sleeve. Bruno kept his attention on Scott and growled as well. Her muscles tightened. She felt the brush of Princess' tiny body against her shin. Then suddenly the small dog began to snarl and bark at the two much larger dogs.

"Princess no!" Nikki swept her up in her arms to protect her. In the middle of all of the commotion she heard a car squeal to a stop beside the sidewalk, a few feet away.

Nikki looked over and recognized the sharp eyes and determined demeanor of her boyfriend Quinn, a police detective with the Dahlia Police Department.

"Quinn!" She called out to him as he jogged towards her. He was followed by two police officers.

"Nikki! What's going on?" Quinn paused inches away from the man on the ground, and the two dogs.

"Marlo's dead!" Gavin exclaimed as he pointed to Marlo's shop.

"These dogs are attacking me! They're going to kill me!" Scott hollered, then yelped, as Rocky growled again.

Quinn's eyes narrowed, as he assessed the situation. His focus remained on the two German Shepherds.

"Marlo's in his shop! He's dead." Gavin looked at Quinn. Quinn gestured for the officers to enter the shop. "I'm pretty sure Scott's the one who did it!"

"I'm not!" Scott shrieked as Rocky tugged at his sleeve. "Let go!"

"Release!" Quinn snapped sharply at Rocky.

The dog instantly released Scott's sleeve, and sat back on his haunches. He looked up at Quinn with what appeared to be a smile.

Quinn turned his attention to Bruno and spoke in the same commanding tone.

"Down!" Bruno sat, then gazed up at Quinn

with his tongue hanging out of the corner of his mouth.

"Good boys, good boys." Quinn took Rocky's leash from Nikki. "Come." He gestured to the sidewalk beside him.

Rocky trotted calmly over to the spot and sat down on the sidewalk. Quinn handed the leash back to Nikki. He met her eyes as he did.

"Are you hurt?"

"No, I'm fine." Nikki stared at him, breathless, as she wondered how he'd worked such magic with the two dogs that refused to listen to her.

Quinn turned his attention back to Scott as he started to get to his feet. He helped him up. Scott edged fearfully away from the dogs.

"Keep those monsters away from me!"

"They won't hurt you now." Quinn eyed the tattered sleeve that hung from his arm. "Did he bite you?"

"No, he just ripped my sleeve and stood on top of me." Scott slipped his fingers through the holes in his sleeve and shook his head. "But I thought he was going to."

"You need to stay here." Quinn ordered. "The officers will question you."

"I didn't do anything!" Scott's eyes widened, his voice grew high pitched. "You have to believe me!"

"I'm going to sort everything out, Scott. We just need to ask you some questions." Quinn nodded.

"Oh yeah?" Scott glared at Gavin. "He's the one you should be questioning. He's the one that's dangerous!"

"What?" Gavin's face grew red with anger. "That's not true!"

"Relax Gavin." Quinn nodded. "We're going to figure all of this out."

As a few more patrol cars pulled up to the scene, Quinn turned Scott and Gavin over to one of the other officers with a brief explanation.

"He took off the moment he saw me! I think he must have been hiding when I went into the shop." Gavin insisted as he pointed at Scott.

"I am going inside." Quinn turned to two officers that had just arrived on the scene. "You wait out here." He walked past Nikki into the shop.

"Marlo's dead in the shop." Gavin shook his head. "He's been stabbed. He's behind the counter."

"What?" Nikki's eyes widened.

"He's behind the counter," Gavin repeated, blinking, as if he couldn't quite believe what he had seen.

Seconds later Quinn stepped back out and relayed orders to his officers.

"We need to seal off the area. Get the medical examiner over here fast." He delivered a few other instructions to the officers, then stepped back inside the shop.

Nikki tried to process what Gavin had said and the events of the morning. Her arm ached a bit from hitting the ground when Scott ran into her, but the pain was overshadowed by the chaos of the unfolding events.

"Nikki?" Quinn called out. "Nikki?"

The sound of Quinn's voice made Nikki snap back to reality.

"Yes." Nikki shook her head as if to clear the fog, "Sorry, I was lost in thought."

"That's okay." Quinn nodded. "You need to give your statement to the officer." He gestured to the officer next to him.

"Okay." Nikki watched Quinn walk over to Gavin, then she turned to the officer and relayed the events of the morning to him. Just as she had finished up, Quinn walked over to them.

"Just finished, sir." The officer turned to Quinn.

"Thank you." Quinn smiled. "Can you help out inside, please."

The officer nodded then walked towards the shop.

"You need to get out of here." Quinn looked into Nikki's eyes.

"Okay." Nikki held tightly to the dogs' leashes. "Are you going to arrest Scott?"

"I don't know, yet." Quinn frowned. "You should get home. Okay?"

"Okay," Nikki mumbled, as Quinn walked off.

"Do you want a ride somewhere?" Another officer leaned closer to her. "Are you sure you're okay to walk?"

"I'm fine, thanks." Nikki sent one more glance over her shoulder, then walked down the sidewalk, away from the shop. Her heart skipped a beat as the events of the morning played through her mind. Logically, the best choice was to continue on and take the dogs home. But with each step she took away from the shop, her sense of logic faded. After what she'd just witnessed, she couldn't just walk away. She needed to see what else she could find out about what happened to Marlo.

As Nikki turned back to the crime scene, she saw Quinn with Scott. Though she couldn't hear the conversation she could tell from the way Quinn leaned close, and Scott stared back at him that the exchange was intense. Gavin stood a few feet from them, listening intently.

Too curious to let it go, Nikki crept closer.

"You can go for the moment." Quinn looked at Scott.

"What are you doing?" Gavin's eyes widened. "Why are you letting him go?"

"Gavin, step back please." Quinn shot him a brief but stern look.

Scott looked towards Gavin and noticed Nikki standing there with the dogs.

"Keep those vicious dogs away from me!" Scott backed away from the dogs, then turned and jogged off down the sidewalk.

Rocky gave a low growl but remained still at Nikki's side. Bruno kept his eyes focused on Quinn.

"Quinn, why are you letting him go?" Nikki held tightly to the leashes.

Quinn frowned, then guided her away from the other officers.

"Listen to me, Nikki, I told you it would be best if you went home, didn't I?"

"Yes, but I needed to see what you found. Why are you releasing him?" Nikki's mind spun.

"Gavin said that he thought Scott was hiding out the back and then came out when he found the body, but it looks like Gavin got to the shop first. My officers interviewed a few shop owners and Gavin was seen walking down the street by a couple of them. He got to the shop a few seconds before Scott pulled up. I don't think that either would have had time to kill Marlo. But I will question them both further of course and see if there are other possible scenarios that would mean that they could have committed the crime. Or if there is any other evidence indicating their guilt." Quinn placed his hands in his pockets and met her eyes. "There's no evidence to indicate that either of them had anything to do with the murder."

"But Scott ran. He was running away from the crime scene." Nikki shook her head. "Why would he run if he had nothing to hide?"

"Maybe because he saw his boss dead?" Quinn shrugged. "Maybe because he saw Gavin staring at Marlo's body, and he didn't know what was happening? He claims he thought Gavin was the killer, and he ran because he thought Gavin would attack him next. Then you and the dogs chased him down and restrained him." He spoke each word emphatically. "I let him go because I have nothing to hold him on."

"Oh wow." Nikki nodded. "I hadn't even

considered what he saw. I just assumed that he had something to do with it because he ran, and because of what Gavin said. I never thought about him being afraid."

"The officers are going to question Gavin and Scott more down at the station." Quinn nodded.

"What about the staff?" Nikki asked. "Are they okay? Are they inside?"

"Apparently, the counter and shop were empty when Gavin got there." Quinn shrugged.

"Really, I don't think I've ever found it empty. Usually Ethel or Pam are at the register, waiting to serve customers." Nikki shook her head. She double-checked the neon sign in the window which declared the shop open. "I don't think I've ever been in there without one of them at the counter and often there's a queue out the door."

"I know." Quinn locked his eyes to Nikki's. "You need to leave this alone. You need to go home." He sighed. "You went through a shock, and you need to rest. Okay? Don't make me insist on an escort."

"I have an escort." Nikki glanced down at the three dogs at her feet. "I think they've made it pretty clear that they will get me home safe."

"Where did the German Shepherds come from?" Quinn gazed at them with some interest.

"What's going on here?" A tall, slender woman emerged from a cab before it even had the chance to come to a full stop. "Who is in charge here? Why is the shop blocked off?"

Nikki's throat grew dry as she recognized the woman from her visits to Marlo's shop.

"That's Carolyn, Marlo's sister." Nikki winced as she took a step back. "They were very close I think, they even worked together. She's not going to take this news easily."

Quinn drew a deep breath, then focused his attention on Carolyn.

Nikki drew the dogs back from Quinn as Carolyn walked up to him.

"Can you please tell me what is going on here? Where is my brother?" Carolyn craned her neck in an attempt to see past the parade of police officers going in and out of the shop. "Marlo?"

"Carolyn." Quinn put one hand gently on her shoulder. "I'm sorry to tell you this, but your brother has passed away."

"What?" Carolyn yanked away from his touch and glared at him. "Have you lost your mind? How dare you play a joke like this!"

"It's not a joke." Quinn straightened his shoulders as he studied her. "He was murdered."

"You're serious?" Carolyn grabbed onto his arm as her entire body swayed forward. "Marlo's dead?"

"Can I get a medic over here?" Quinn summoned one of the paramedics that lingered near the scene. He caught Carolyn gently around the waist, just in time to keep her from collapsing.

Two paramedics ran over with a gurney between them. Quinn helped to ease Carolyn onto the gurney.

"I am sorry for your loss. I know this is a shock, but if there is anything you can tell me about what your brother did this morning, or anyone he may have had a problem with, then please do. The sooner we get that information, the better the chances are of us finding out who did this to your brother."

She wriggled free of their grasp and sat up to look straight at Quinn.

"You need to find out who did this." Carolyn scowled at him as the paramedics rolled her towards the ambulance. "Do your job, Detective!" She swung her legs over the edge of the gurney. "Let me off of this thing right now. No one is taking me anywhere!" As she jumped down from the gurney, the paramedics scrambled to prevent her from falling.

Steady on her feet, Carolyn charged right towards the door of Marlo's shop. "I want to see him! I want to see my brother right now!"

Quinn managed to catch her around the waist just before she could get through the door.

"I can't let you in there, Carolyn."

"Let me go! Right this second!" Carolyn swung her arms wildly at Quinn.

"Stop now!" Another officer ran up to the pair.

Nikki gasped as she saw him reach for his gun.

"It's okay." Quinn ducked one of Carolyn's blows and glared at the officer. "It's okay, back off."

The officer hesitated, then followed Quinn's command.

"Carolyn." Nikki touched her shoulder and tried to meet her eyes. "Please Carolyn, the police have to do their investigation to find out what happened."

Carolyn spun around to face her.

"I'm so sorry for your loss, Carolyn." Nikki bit into her bottom lip.

"He was all I had." Carolyn cried as Nikki held the leashes with one hand and put her other arm around Carolyn's shoulders.

"The police are going to find out what happened to him." Nikki squeezed Carolyn's shoulders. "It may not be much comfort, but they will find out."

"You better find who did this. Do you hear me?" Carolyn pulled away from Nikki and shot a glare in Quinn's direction as tears streamed down her face.

"Yes, I hear you." Quinn met her eyes. "I will keep you up to date with the investigation. But if you have any further information, it would be helpful to have it now, while it's fresh in your mind. Could we talk?" He gestured to a table and chairs outside of one of the nearby shops.

"Yes, we can talk." Carolyn walked over to the table.

Quinn followed after her.

Nikki studied the pair for a few moments, then guided the dogs back down the sidewalk. Her heart still racing from the events of the morning.

CHAPTER 3

*A*lthough the two larger dogs had appeared very protective and riled up not long before, as they strolled down the sidewalk ahead of Nikki, they remained calm. Nikki kept a close eye on Princess who walked a few paces behind the dogs.

Nikki heard more sirens as more officers gathered at Marlo's shop. She glanced across the street and spotted Nathan, the manager of Chop Chop Butcher Shop, standing outside on the sidewalk. He stared down the street at the gathering in front of Marlo's shop.

Nikki's heart sank as she wondered if Nathan had heard the news, yet. Would he be thrilled that his competition had been eliminated? She pushed away the thought and focused her attention instead on the sidewalk ahead of her. The rivalry between Chop Chop and Marlo's shop had become fierce in the past few weeks.

As Nikki crossed into the residential area of town, she considered the possibility that Nathan could have had something to do with the murder. No matter how she tried to ignore the idea, her thoughts returned to it. Who else in town would have something against Marlo? It made her uneasy to even consider it. When she'd first seen Scott run from the shop, with Gavin insisting that Scott was the murderer, she had instantly assumed that was the case. But with what Quinn had discovered, she couldn't be certain of that.

Nikki headed straight for Sonia's house, eager to get Princess home before Sonia started worrying why they were out for so long. She did not look forward to the conversation she would have with Petra about Rocky and Bruno. She knew that she would have to give her some details about what happened, just in case Scott decided to make a fuss about it.

"Nikki!" Sonia waved to her from the end of her

driveway. "I was about to call you. I just heard what happened. It's all around town. Is it true that Rocky and Bruno attacked someone?"

"Is that all that you heard?" Nikki met Sonia's eyes.

"All I know is that there are tons of cops around Marlo's, and that people saw one of the dogs tackle someone." Sonia picked Princess up and eyed the two dogs that sat down beside Nikki. "Is it true? Do you think they are dangerous?"

"Rocky did tackle someone." Nikki frowned as she looked down at the perfectly content dog. "But only because the man ran into me and he was being protective, I think. He didn't cause any harm to the person. He just stopped him from running away. Something worse happened, actually." She glanced up and down the street to be sure that no one else stood close enough to overhear her. "Marlo is dead!"

"What?" Sonia gasped, then clamped her hand over her mouth.

Nikki explained the events of the morning.

"Wow!" Sonia's eyes widened. "You've had quite a morning. Were you hurt?"

"No, not really, my arm is a bit sore. Gavin thought that Scott had something to do with the murder. Apparently, he wanted to make sure he didn't get away. I don't know, maybe Rocky sensed that and got alarmed when he knocked me over." Nikki looked down at the dog again.

"Maybe Scott really did have something to do with it." Sonia clutched Princess close against her chest.

"Maybe, but maybe Gavin really was the murderer and he is trying to divert attention from himself by directing it at Scott." Nikki bit into her bottom lip and shifted from one foot to the other. "Now, I have to go drop off the dogs at Petra's and let her know what happened. If only I had held tighter to Rocky's leash. But my arm was a bit sore from the fall."

"Scott barreled into you. Rocky's a strong dog, Nikki." Sonia smiled slightly. "I'm sure that Petra will understand."

"I hope so." Nikki glanced down the road in the direction of Petra's home. "I should get going. I need to be back to the shelter in time to help with the mid-day walks."

"Take it easy, Nikki." Sonia gave her a quick hug. "Maybe you should just take the afternoon off and head home. Or you could stay here."

"Don't worry about me, Sonia." Nikki took a

deep breath then forced a smile. "I will be fine. I'm sure that Quinn will get to the bottom of this quickly."

"Poor Marlo." Sonia sighed. "What a shame. He worked so hard to build that business. Oh dear, and what about his sister?"

"She knows. She's heartbroken." Nikki's heart pounded at the thought. "I wish there was something I could do to help."

"Maybe we'll think of something." Sonia looked into her eyes. "We can take up a collection for her, or maybe have a special event in Marlo's honor. We'll figure something out."

"Those are great ideas." Nikki nodded, her mind still spinning from the entire experience. "I'll touch base with you later. It was amazing how Princess kept up with the other dogs. I'm sure she could use some rest and extra cuddling."

"I'll make sure she gets it." Sonia buried her cheek in the dog's soft fur.

Nikki smiled, then continued down the street. Although there was about a fifty-year age gap between them, Sonia and Nikki had become close friends and Sonia always had a way of getting to the point, and reassuring Nikki.

Nikki crossed the street between the wealthier

houses and the working-class neighborhood. The homes transformed from sprawling mansions into ranchers and two-story single-family homes. Many had Christmas decorations in their front yards. A little farther down the street, she saw the green rancher that belonged to Rocky and Bruno, at least for the moment.

The two dogs quickened their pace. She guessed that they recognized that they were almost home. She braced herself for Petra's reaction. Would she be angry with her? She had every right to be.

As Nikki approached the front door, Rocky gave a jovial bark and hopped up to put his paws on the door.

The door swung open, and Petra stood in the doorway. Her eyes lit up at the sight of the dogs.

"Hi babies!" She grinned as she crouched down to greet them.

Both dogs rushed forward to get a pat. Neither showed any indication of being aggressive.

"Hi Petra." Nikki took a deep breath, then she launched into a description of what happened.

"You're sure?" Petra's eyes widened. "Neither of the dogs has ever exhibited any kind of behavior like that before. But I've only had them for a couple of days."

"I think they just reacted on instinct. The whole thing was pretty chaotic. Or maybe they thought I was in danger." Nikki frowned as she shook her head. "I take full responsibility for what happened. I'm very sorry. As far as I know, as of now, a complaint about the dogs hasn't been made, but it is possible that it still will be."

"Oh Nikki, I'm sure it will be okay." Petra straightened up.

"I hope so."

After dropping the dogs off, Nikki headed back to the shelter and arrived just in time to take the dogs for their mid-day walk. As she walked the streets near the shelter, she thought about Gavin's accusations of Scott. Did Gavin really think that Scott was the killer when he saw him? Maybe he was. Or maybe Gavin was? Quinn seemed to think that neither could have committed the crime because of the time frame but maybe he was missing something. She did her best to recall everything she had learned that day. Had Marlo fought with someone in the shop? Where were all the other employees?

Nikki sighed as she made her way back towards the shelter. No matter how she tried to picture it, Marlo's murder just didn't make sense to her. Maybe he had his moments, but as far as she knew he was a kind and generous man who was always willing to work with someone or make a deal. She couldn't picture anyone that would want him dead.

"How about a break, pups?" Nikki gave each one a pat on the head, then sat down on the bench. She pulled her phone out of her pocket and began to search for information about Marlo. She scrolled through an assortment of advertisements, a few politically charged comments on a local page, and some rants from unhappy customers. She skimmed over those. Most were complaints about him raising prices, one was a complaint about the temperature in his shop. But the last one drew her attention.

Marlo can't be trusted. I taught him everything he knows, and what did he do to thank me? He framed me in an attempt to make me lose my business. He made it out to seem as if I have a dirty shop, but the only dirty one around here, is Marlo. No love lost there.

Nikki frowned as she read over the comment again. Marlo had mentioned to her that he had been fired from another butcher shop, and that had caused him to start his own business. She wondered if the comment might have come from his previous employer.

After a little more searching, Nikki was able to confirm that the comment was posted by Philip Ardoine, the owner of Meat Stop, which still operated in Fuchsia, the next town over. The animosity in the comment made Nikki certain that Philip held a grudge against Marlo, and maybe for good reason. Had Marlo gotten revenge on his former boss somehow? Had his former boss decided to get him back?

Nikki was about to dial the number for Meat Stop, when her cell phone began to ring. She smiled at the sight of Quinn's name and answered the call.

"I'm so glad you called." Nikki stood up from the bench. "Are you doing okay?"

"I will be, when I see you. Dinner tonight?" Quinn's tone brightened.

"Sure, I'll pick up something. I'm sure neither of us wants to cook." Nikki cringed. The last thing she wanted to do was cook.

"Great, thanks hon. I'll see you tonight."

"Anything new in the investigation?" Nikki led the dogs along the sidewalk.

"Nothing solid, yet. I'm working on it."

"I know you are. See you tonight."

Nikki ended the call and slid her phone into her pocket. After she dropped off the dogs at the shelter, she drove towards the address in Fuchsia listed for Meat Stop. The owner could easily hang up on her if she called. It would be harder to turn her away in person. Plus, she wanted to see his reaction to the news of Marlo's murder. Nikki was always surprised when her car started on the first go. She knew she would need to replace it soon, but money was tight, and the mechanic always managed to fix it to keep it going for a while before it gave trouble again.

Nikki parked in the parking lot in front of Meat Stop and made her way to the front door. An assortment of large posters advertising special discounts hung in the front window. She pulled open the door and stepped inside. Everything hanging in the front window blocked out most of the sunlight, which left the interior of the shop dim. Although fluorescent lights flickered over the front counter, they struggled to spread light.

A short man behind the counter glanced over at her. His eyebrows were thick and stuck out in strange directions. Similar tufts of hair poked out from under the sleeves of his tight t-shirt and grew in scraggly strands from his chest. Black glasses framed his stern, brown eyes as he studied her.

"May I help you?"

"I would like some bones, please." Nikki paused in front of the counter.

"Bones. What type?" He brushed a hand across a surprisingly thin mustache.

"Do you have any bones available for dogs? I'm a dog walker, and I need a couple for one of my dogs." Nikki smiled as she watched a hint of a smile touch his lips.

"Oh, I see. I may have a few. I'll check in the back." He walked through the door into the back.

Alone in the front of the shop, Nikki took in every detail she could. However, she didn't notice anything that stood out as strange. She had no idea what she was even looking for. Then her eyes landed on a photograph on the wall. It appeared to be an assortment of Meat Stop employees. Beside the photograph was a newspaper article proclaiming Meat Stop the best butcher shop in the state. The date on the article was from a few years before. Nikki looked back at the photograph and noticed Marlo front and center. Philip's arm draped around the younger man's shoulders. It appeared to her that they were far closer than just boss and employee.

"Here you are." Philip stepped through the door and set a container on the counter. "Is this what you're looking for?"

Nikki eyed the bones in the container. They were huge.

"You don't have anything smaller?"

"No, this is all I have." Phillip spoke gruffly as he snatched the container back.

"I see, they're a bit big for him. That's all right." Nikki cleared her throat and braced herself as she decided to bring up the topic of Marlo. "I had placed an order with Marlo's Butcher Shoppe, but after what happened this morning, I don't think I'll be getting my order."

The container slipped out of Philip's hand and hit the floor. He spun around to face her.

"What about Marlo?"

"Do you know him?" Nikki's muscles tightened as she looked straight into his eyes.

"I do." Philip narrowed his eyes. "What happened?"

"I am sorry to say that he passed away this morning. He was murdered." Nikki's mind flashed back to the events of the morning. She tried to imagine Philip killing him. Marlo was a good bit taller, and at least fifty pounds heavier. Could he have overpowered the larger man? She studied Philip's face as his eyes widened and he looked away. A soft sound escaped his lips, not quite a cough and not exactly a gasp.

CHAPTER 4

"Sir?" Nikki took a step closer to the counter to get a better look at him. "Are you okay?"

"No." Philip turned back to look at her. "No, I'm not." His eyes remained wide, but dry.

"I'm sorry, were you two friends?" Nikki glanced around the shop. "Being in the same business I guess you crossed paths."

"He was a confused young man." Phillip's eyes narrowed. "A very confused young man."

"I'm sorry for your loss." Nikki memorized the words he spoke.

"I lost him a long time ago." Phillip shook his head as he picked the container up off the floor. "I hope you're able to find your bones, young lady. Now, if you don't mind, I have some work to do."

"Of course." Nikki watched as he disappeared into the back. There was no doubt in her mind that he had a close relationship with Marlo at some point, but was his reaction to Marlo's death just an act? If he had been the one to kill him, then he certainly wouldn't have been shocked to hear about his death. Could he have killed Marlo and then just continued on with his day?

Nikki snapped a quick picture of the photograph on the wall, then left the shop. As she settled in her car, she drew a few deep breaths to relax her nerves. She had no idea how to read Philip's reaction to Marlo's death. But his comment about losing Marlo a long time ago made her think things were still bad between them. She needed more information about their relationship.

Carolyn. Nikki started the car. She's going to be the one who knows about Marlo's past. She pulled out her phone and did a quick search for Carolyn's information. Although she stumbled across a few social media pages with Carolyn's name, and pictures here and there, none included her current address or phone number. She searched for information about Marlo's business. He and a few employees were listed, but Carolyn's name did not appear on anything related to the business. Frustrated, she decided to turn her attention to the employees that were missing from the shop that morning. Where were they at the time of the murder?

Pam and Ethel were both familiar to Nikki, but she knew Ethel a little better than Pam, as she had cared for her Dandie Dinmont Terrier, Percy, while she traveled south to care for her ailing mother. Instead of calling her, she decided to drive to her house. She guessed that if Ethel was upset about what happened, she might not answer her phone, but it would be harder for her to turn Nikki away face to face.

As Nikki drove to the familiar address, she wondered how she would find Ethel. The older woman had a stern personality, but in the face of this tragedy Nikki doubted that she would be so stoic. She parked in the driveway behind Ethel's station wagon and walked up to the front door. Just before she knocked, she felt a pang of guilt carry through her. Was it right to disturb her after such a terrible thing had happened?

Nikki started to lower her hand, then recalled her promise to Carolyn. If she wanted to help find out what happened to Marlo, she had to ask the hard questions, while everything would still be fresh. After a swift knock, the door swung open.

"Oh, it's you." Ethel stared straight at Nikki with an indifferent expression.

"Hi Ethel." Nikki cleared her throat, startled by the woman's calm exterior. "I just wanted to check on you. I know that you must be so upset about what happened this morning."

"About Marlo?" Ethel shrugged. "We're all going to die, aren't we?"

"Well, yes." Nikki shifted from one foot to the other and looked away for a moment. "How is Percy doing?"

"He's just fine. And so am I." Ethel rolled her eyes. "People get so caught up in things that are none of their business."

"It's just that I was there just after Marlo was found." Nikki allowed her voice to tremble a little. "It was so shocking."

"I'm sure it was." Ethel reached out and gave her a light pat on her shoulder. "There, is that better?"

Nikki took a slight step back as she studied the woman. She'd always known her to be gruff, but this seemed a little extreme.

"Actually, what would be better is knowing a little bit more about Marlo. I thought maybe you could help me with that?"

"Like I said, I like to mind my own business." Ethel tipped her head to the side. "But what do you want to know?"

"He used to work over at Meat Stop, right?" Nikki noticed a subtle shift in Ethel's expression.

"Yeah, he did." Ethel coughed. "What about it?"

"I came across a complaint about Marlo, written by the owner of Meat Stop that said Marlo couldn't be trusted. Do you know anything about that?" Nikki looked straight into her eyes.

Ethel blinked. Then she looked away. Her shoulders slumped just enough to soften her stance.

"I don't know much about that, no. Marlo had nothing good to say about Philip, though. I guess, Philip accused him of setting him up to lose his business." Ethel shrugged. "What does that matter now?"

"Do you think Philip might have still been angry with Marlo?" Nikki raised an eyebrow.

"Are you asking me if Philip might have killed Marlo?" Ethel laughed, loud and hard. Her body shook as she leaned against the doorway. "Are you kidding? Philip? He's the weakest man I've ever met."

"Oh, you've met him?" Nikki took a step closer to her. "Did you know him when he and Marlo worked together?"

"Enough of this." Ethel waved her hand. "I have things to do. Thanks for stopping by." She stepped back into the house.

"Ethel, just one more thing." Nikki caught the door before she could close it. "Why wasn't anyone else working at the shop this morning? Gavin said that when he got there, the door was open, and Marlo was the only person there."

"I have no idea. I was off this morning. Pam was supposed to be working. Betty, the part-time butcher, only worked when Marlo wasn't available, so she wasn't working today." Ethel looked into Nikki's eyes. "Like I said, I don't get into other people's business." She pushed the door closed.

Nikki frowned as she walked back to her car. She guessed that Ethel knew more than she said. But she couldn't force the woman to talk.

As Nikki headed back into town, she caught a glimpse of the time on the dashboard clock. Her heart skipped a beat. It was after six, and she hadn't even thought about dinner. She guessed that Quinn would be on his way home. She stopped by Vito's, the Italian place they both liked, and ordered their favorites. As she waited for the order to be filled, she started to search for information about Pam. She found lots of pictures of her, and as she studied one, she heard someone speak up beside her.

"Just the pizza please, and fast, the kids are starving."

Nikki looked up to see the same person she'd just been looking at.

"Pam?" The name popped out of her mouth.

"Yes?" Pam looked over at Nikki. She looked to be in her late twenties, but the ponytail she wore her long, blonde hair in made her appear a little younger.

"I'm Nikki." She offered her hand to Pam.

"I remember you." Pam offered a half-smile as she shook her hand. "You've been in Marlo's shop a few times."

"Yes." Nikki hesitated. She hadn't had time to plan out what she would ask Pam.

"I, uh, I heard that you were there when Marlo was found." Pam's voice shook as she spoke. Her cheeks flushed. She looked down at the floor.

"I was. I was outside the shop." Nikki bit into her bottom lip.

"I just don't understand." Pam drew a sharp breath. "I just don't know why it happened."

"It's a terrible thing." Nikki gently touched Pam's shoulder. "I know it must be a huge shock to you."

"I can't believe it really. I keep thinking I'll wake up, and all of this will have been a nightmare." Pam handed some cash to the man at the register and accepted a pizza box from him. "I'm sorry, I have to go. My kids are with the sitter and they haven't had dinner."

Nikki's heart pounded as she realized this might be her only chance to ask Pam some questions. She couldn't let it slip away.

"Pam, Ethel mentioned that you were supposed to be working this morning. But when Gavin got to the shop, apparently no one else was there." Nikki met the woman's eyes and noted the tears that had gathered there.

"My daughter, she's two, and she was at daycare, but she got a fever. They told me I had to pick her up. I tried to get my sitter to pick her up, but she wasn't available. I couldn't reach her." Pam's hands trembled as she gripped the pizza box. "I was going to bring her back to the shop until my sitter could pick her up." Her face paled. "We could have been there when it happened."

"I'm very sorry for your loss, Pam." Nikki could see the fear in the woman's eyes.

"Thank you." Pam lowered her eyes, then hurried out of the restaurant.

Nikki paid for her order, then headed back to her car. She guessed that if the daycare had called Pam to pick up her daughter, and the daycare wasn't too far away, the window of time when the murder could have taken place had to be fairly tight. Did someone know that Marlo would be alone? Did they pick that time to murder him?

CHAPTER 5

*N*ikki's mind swirled as she drove to Quinn's house. As she expected, his car was already parked in the driveway.

Nikki parked behind it and stepped out of the car with the takeout food in one hand and her purse in the other. As she walked up to the door, it swung open, and Quinn stepped outside. He met her eyes briefly before he reached for the bag.

"Here, let me take that for you."

"I'm sorry I'm late." Nikki frowned as she handed over the bag. "I lost track of time."

"Don't apologize, it happens." Quinn smiled at her then placed a light kiss on her cheek. "How are you doing?" He led her into the house.

Spots ran up to greet her with sloppy licks on her hands.

"Hi buddy." Nikki crouched down to hug him and kiss him on the top of his head. "Oh, it's so good to see you!"

"Careful, I'm getting jealous." Quinn laughed as he put the bag on the island in the center of the kitchen and opened it up. "Oh yes, I was hoping you went to Vito's."

"I thought you might need a boost after today." Nikki straightened up and walked over to him. She noticed the tension in his shoulders, and that his smile faded when he thought she wasn't looking at him. "Is everything okay?"

"Just a busy day. It's a lot to take in." Quinn glanced over at her. "How are you? Did you go home and rest?"

"I'm doing okay." Nikki tipped her head to the side and scrunched up her nose. "I guess that depends on how you define rest, and home." She raised her eyebrows.

"I see." Quinn smiled as he looked into her eyes. "I didn't think you would. I'll get this all set up in the dining room. Do you want to take Spots out back for me?"

"Sure." Nikki guided the Dalmatian through the

back door into Quinn's expansive backyard. It still surprised her to see just how large it was, lined with a short fence, and trees in the distance. Compared to her apartment, Quinn's house felt like a mansion. As Spots ran across the yard after a speedy squirrel, she took a deep breath of the crisp air. She shoved her hands into her pockets and gazed up at the sky. A few stars had already begun to glimmer.

Lost in thought, sudden arms around her waist made her gasp.

"It's just me." Quinn held her tighter. "I'm sorry, I didn't mean to startle you."

"It's okay." Nikki relaxed and leaned back against his broad chest.

"I know what happened this morning shocked you." Quinn kissed her cheek and nestled his chin against the crook of her shoulder and neck. "You must be tired."

"I'm really not." Nikki pulled away and turned to face him. "I actually want to know every detail that you can share with me about the murder."

"Of course you do." Quinn's eyes narrowed. "I'm guessing you have a lot to fill me in about, too."

"Maybe." Nikki couldn't hide a grin. "Have you looked into Marlo's former employer, Philip?"

"All right, inside." Quinn guided her through the

door with a soft chuckle. Spots pushed past them and rushed straight to his food dish in the kitchen.

"I wanted to get some bones for Spots and so I talked to him today, and I think there's something there, Quinn." Nikki settled in a chair at the table.

"Is that so?" Quinn sat down across from her and picked up the glass of water in front of him. "What did you two talk about?"

"He didn't seem to know that Marlo was dead. When I mentioned it, he got upset, but then he said that he'd lost Marlo a long time ago. Do you know what that's about?" Nikki picked up her glass.

"Actually, I do. I've been looking into their connection. It seems that after Marlo was fired, there were a lot of social media posts about the quality of the meat from Philip's shop. A few had pictures of roaches in the meat. The health inspector inspected the property and a couple of roaches were found. They were closed down for a few days. I spoke to the man who conducted the inspection, and according to him, Philip was convinced that Marlo had made the posts, planted roaches and falsified the pictures." Quinn took a sip of his water as he studied her.

"Ugh, not exactly dinner conversation." Nikki

winced as she popped open the food container in front of her. "Do you think that Marlo set him up?"

"I don't know. What do you think? I didn't get the chance to speak to Philip directly yet, so you might have a better idea of what happened between them." Quinn picked up his fork and dug into the chicken parmigiana in front of him.

"Unfortunately, I don't think I do. He shut down pretty fast once I asked about Marlo." Nikki shrugged and spun some spaghetti around her fork. "I definitely think he was holding a grudge, though."

"So, he may have some motive, but it's a bit extreme to go from firing someone to murdering them." Quinn took a bite and grabbed a napkin to mop some sauce from his chin.

"Do you know why Marlo was fired?" Nikki grinned and used her own napkin to clean up a spot on his chin that he missed.

"I don't. Not yet. I'll speak to Philip tomorrow." Quinn took another bite.

"Why do I feel like there's a lot that you're not telling me?" Nikki poked at her spaghetti.

"Because I don't want you anywhere near this case." Quinn set his fork down and looked straight into her eyes. "Because you spent the whole day going around town, snooping, when I had hoped that you would relax and stay out of it."

"Quinn." Nikki looked right back at him. "Have we just met?"

Quinn sighed and wiped his hand across his face. "Yes, I know, I know. You have a need to get to the truth."

"Is that such a bad thing?" Nikki frowned as she sat back in her chair. "It's not as if it's new."

"I know." Quinn smiled. "We narrowed down the time frame of Marlo's murder. It was going to be hard to pinpoint because of the temperature. But we pinned down the last time Marlo was seen or spoken to." He looked up at her. "From initial tests his time of death was between ten to twenty minutes before Gavin apparently found him. Twenty at the most."

"That's good news isn't it? It means that the crime was discovered quickly, there's a better chance of finding evidence, and narrowing down who the killer could be." Nikki's heart began to race as she mentally reviewed what she knew.

"It's good news, for the investigation." Quinn smiled. "I'm just glad you didn't get there earlier. You might have encountered the killer. I worry about you because you always jump in first and ask questions later."

"I don't think that's true." Nikki frowned.

"I know it is." Quinn smiled as he studied her. "It's something I admire about you. But it also frightens me." His brows knitted. "I just want you to be careful. Okay? I know I can't stop you from looking into things, but please, if you come across something or someone that you think might be risky, run it by me before you do anything. Okay?"

"Okay." Nikki leaned across the table and kissed him. As she sat back, she saw the tension in his features had only relaxed a little. "Let's try that again." She kissed him again.

Quinn sighed through the kiss and ran his fingers back through her hair.

"Better?" Nikki sat back in her chair and looked into his eyes.

"The best." Quinn smiled. "It's almost as if you care about me or something."

"I do." Nikki grinned.

"You're sure?" Quinn raised an eyebrow.

"Absolutely."

"And there's nothing I could say right now that would change that?" Quinn's eyes narrowed.

"What is it?" Nikki braced herself.

"So, this year, I thought it might be nice if

everyone was together for Christmas." Quinn licked his lips.

"Oh, that's a sweet thought." Nikki smiled, then took a sip of her water. "But everyone's so busy, and so scattered."

"Don't worry about that." Quinn held her gaze. "I made all of the arrangements. My parents, your parents, Kyle, they're all going to be here. And, of course Mrs. Whitter."

"Wait, what?" Nikki's heart dropped as she searched his eyes. "Are you serious?"

"Yes, I thought it would be a nice surprise." Quinn winced. "Is it?"

"Is it?" Nikki took a sharp breath as her heartbeat quickened. All of their family smashed together for a holiday? She knew the time was coming, but was she really ready for it? Were they? "Of course it is." She cleared her throat, then took another, larger sip of her water. "Even Kyle?"

"Even Kyle. He said he's looking forward to it. I thought we could host the dinner here, if that's all right with you? I know you are flat out at the moment. I'm on shift during the day and you're helping at the shelter all week. I can have it catered. So, neither of us will have to worry about our cooking skills." Quinn shifted in his chair as he gazed at her. "Sounds good, right?"

"Perfect." Nikki set her glass down a bit harder than she intended.

"Are you ever going to stop doing that?" Quinn sat forward and pushed his glass out of the way so that he could reach for her hand.

"Doing what?" Nikki pushed the panic from her mind and tried to focus on his words. She could tell from the determination in his eyes that he wasn't going to let the idea in his head rest.

"Saying what you think I want to hear?" Quinn sighed as he wrapped his fingers around hers. "Don't you know that you can be honest with me?"

"I am being." Nikki lowered her eyes. "I just need to sort through things sometimes. I'm not always sure what to say."

"It's okay to tell me that, too." Quinn brushed his thumb across the back of her hand. "I know, I went behind your back on this. I only did that because I didn't want you to be disappointed if I couldn't get everyone on board. But if that bothers you, if this whole plan bothers you, I can cancel it."

"It doesn't bother me, it's just a surprise." Nikki rested her chin on her hand and gazed at him. "I think it's wonderful that you did all of this. It's just a shock. And, an adjustment."

"I promise, it's all going to go smoothly. I'll make sure that everything is taken care of and we can just enjoy some time with our families. I'm really looking forward to getting to spend some time with Kyle, and my mother has been dying to meet you properly. She hasn't seen you since we were at school." Quinn smiled. "Don't worry, she's harmless. Mostly."

"Now, I'm worried." Nikki laughed and squeezed his hand. "I can't wait to meet her and your father as well. I'm sure it will be wonderful." She winked. "How did I get so lucky?"

"I'm the lucky one." Quinn looked up at the ceiling, then shook his head. "I just hope this case is settled before then. It's shaping up to be a difficult one. Even with the narrow time of death."

"Did you get much from Carolyn?" Nikki tipped her head to the side.

"No. I tried to question her, but she clammed up. I barely got any information from her." Quinn frowned.

"You know that's funny, because I was trying to find some information about her today, after I spoke to Philip. I thought if I could find her number or address, I could talk to her about Marlo's relationship with Philip. But when I looked for it, I couldn't find it. Marlo mentioned that she had come to help out with the business side of things, like advertising. But I even dug into the business records of Marlo's shop, and I was surprised to see that her name isn't listed on any business records. At least from what I could find." Nikki took another bite of her spaghetti and talked around it. "It's odd, don't you think?"

"I ran into the same situation. Although, I do have her phone number. She said she doesn't have a permanent address, yet. She's been staying at Marlo's apartment until she finds a place of her own. I have one of my guys digging further into her to see if we can get a better handle on her, but so far, he hasn't come up with much. She is a private person with not much social media presence, like many people. She's only recently started working at Marlo's business." Quinn pointed his fork at her. "Sometimes it's good to let the police do their job, you know?"

"I know." Nikki grinned. "Hopefully, she'll open up about it, because I hit a brick wall with her. She's going to be the key to finding out more about Marlo's past. Without that, how can you know who else might have been holding a grudge against him? Oh, and I spoke to Ethel today, she's a strange one."

"Wow, you were as busy as me." Quinn rolled his eyes and smiled. "I spoke to Ethel, too. She is definitely odd. But I didn't come up with anything that made me think she was involved. Did you?"

"No, not exactly. But like you mentioned about the time of death being such a tight time frame, I feel like someone had to know that Marlo was alone there. Otherwise the murderer probably wouldn't have taken the risk of killing him in the shop." Nikki shrugged.

"You're assuming that the crime was premeditated. If Marlo had an argument with someone, perhaps the killer just lost it and killed him." Quinn scrunched up his nose as he looked down at his food. "Also, not dinner conversation, I guess."

"What about Gavin? Did his alibi check out?" Nikki asked.

"Yes, he has a solid alibi. He was at work and walked straight from there to Marlo's shop. I have eyewitnesses that can vouch for his presence from six in the morning. There is no way he could have committed the crime from what I can tell."

"And Scott had nothing to say?" Nikki met his eyes. "Does he have a solid alibi?"

"Not as solid as Gavin's. He claims he was out on deliveries all morning, and that he had only seen Marlo for a bit when the shop opened this morning and he picked up the deliveries." Quinn rubbed his cheek. "For such a bold murder, in an open shop, in the middle of the morning, we don't have a lot to go on."

"I'm sure something will turn up." Nikki leaned back in her chair and closed her eyes, then suddenly sat forward. "What about the dogs? Did Scott file a complaint?"

"No, I pointed out that he wasn't hurt, and that the moment was just a very chaotic one. I think I convinced him that it would be best to let it go." Quinn pursed his lips for a moment, then met her eyes. "What do you know about those dogs?"

"Not much. Petra's friend was pet sitting them for the holidays, but he broke his leg, so Petra is taking care of them until their owners come home." Nikki shook her head. "I should have held tighter to that leash. But Rocky wouldn't listen to me. It was strange how he responded so quickly to you. Maybe they had a male owner previously."

"Actually, I think it might be more specific than

that. When I was in the academy, I trained with some police dogs. We learned the commands they're trained with. That's what I used to get the dog to let go of Scott. I think they might be former police dogs."

"Wow." Nikki's eyes widened at the thought. "I'll have to ask Petra about it, but when I mentioned what happened she didn't say anything about that."

"Now, enough about the case." Quinn offered his hand to her. "I have about ten minutes before I need to get back to work, and I want to spend it under the stars with you."

Nikki smiled as they put on their coats and he led her out onto the porch swing. Spots jumped up into their laps. He lay across both of them. Quinn pulled a blanket from the side of the swing and covered their legs. For the few minutes they had together Nikki drifted on the swing beside him. Just his nearness was enough to help her to relax and close her eyes.

Quinn kissed the top of her head.

"I should get home." Nikki stretched as she stood up. Spots jumped off when she moved. "Sorry, buddy." She bent down to give him a kiss and a pat on his head then stood back up.

"I'll call you in the morning." Quinn stood up

and took her hand. "If you can't sleep, text me." His dark blue eyes took her breath away as they stared into hers. He kissed her on the lips, then watched as she walked towards her car.

Nikki felt a rush of excitement at the thought of their families meeting and enjoying the holidays together, but the rush faded as she settled into bed. How could she look forward to something so joyful, when Marlo's family had been torn apart? She needed to help find his murderer.

CHAPTER 6

*N*ikki woke up the next morning, well aware of the fact that Christmas was one day closer. She'd been so caught up in everything that happened the day before, she had missed out on quite a few things on her to-do list. Still, the festivities of the holiday didn't seem so important when compared to Marlo's murder. His sister wouldn't be able to celebrate it with him, and someone needed to be held accountable for that.

Nikki climbed out of bed and took a quick shower. As her mind relaxed, her thoughts returned to the events of the previous day. She hadn't had much of a chance to look around yesterday. She'd been so shocked by Marlo's murder and the chaos after, that she'd forgotten to look for clues that might reveal more about the murderer. She decided that she would do her best to get a look at Marlo's shop. With the police done with their initial search of the shop, she hoped it would be closed and she might be able to sneak in to take a look around.

Nikki first stopped to pick up Rocky and Bruno. Petra had given her the keys to pick them up and drop them off. They panted their greetings at her the moment she opened the door. She grinned and gave them each a good pet. As she looked into each of their eager eyes, she saw no trace of the animosity they'd displayed the day before. Maybe Quinn was right. Maybe they had been police dogs. She decided she would ask Petra if she had found out more about them the first chance she had.

Instead of heading straight to Sonia's to pick up Princess, Nikki decided to walk through town so that she could have a look at Marlo's shop. The cheerful holiday decorations that covered most of the trees, and lined the streets, reminded her of that to-do list she'd been neglecting. Now that she knew that her family and Quinn's family would be in town for Christmas, she had even more to do to get prepared. As she walked past the hardware store, she remembered that she wanted to get some things to hang up some Christmas decorations at the animal shelter. She pulled open the door to the hardware store and stepped inside. Uncertain of the dogs' behavior in stores, she kept them both on a short leash.

As Nikki waved to Gus Right, the owner of the store, she noticed a man at the counter that she didn't recognize. He looked to be in his seventies with a bald head and bushy, gray beard.

"All I'm saying is that if we had a decent police force in this town, maybe that murder never would have happened. It seems like every time I turn around, someone is up to something that they shouldn't be. If I can see it, then why can't the police?" He shook his head. "It's downright ridiculous. Our taxes pay for their salaries. And what do they do? Sit around in their cars waiting to write tickets. So, we have to pay more, while they do nothing to prevent crime here. Dahlia used to be a decent place to live you know. When I was a boy, no one had to lock their doors. No one was worried about walking around at night, and no one had to worry about opening their shop up in the morning. You have no idea how much I worry about my boy. Every day he is at risk. I've tried to warn him about the things going on in this town, but I'm not sure he completely understands."

"I get what you're saying, but every town has its ups and downs, John." Gus shook his head and popped open the cash register. "If you're that concerned about it, you can always go to a town meeting." He handed John his change and pushed his bag across the counter towards him. "Personally, I've never had any trouble with crime or the police."

"Sure, you haven't. What about that break-in last summer?" John pointed his finger at him. "I don't forget these things so easily."

"That was just a couple of kids trying to steal some tools." Gus shrugged and gave a short laugh. "I can't blame them for doing the same things I did as a kid."

"But if the police were more vigilant, then they never would have gotten as far as breaking your window and getting into the storage room." John pursed his lips as he grabbed the bag.

"Or maybe if I had actually turned on my alarm before I left that night?" Gus winced and scratched the back of his neck. "I haven't forgotten since that day. It was a good lesson for me actually, and luckily it only cost me the price of a new window. If the police hadn't noticed their flashlights inside the shop, they might have gotten away with the tools."

"You're missing the point." John sighed. "The point is, it never should have been able to happen in the first place. You just don't understand."

"Maybe I don't." Gus glanced briefly at Nikki, then looked back at John. "You've given me a lot to think about, though."

"Not enough I'm afraid." John sighed.

Nikki finished grabbing the items she needed and did her best to keep her mouth shut. She had a lot to say about John's opinion of the police force, but she knew it wouldn't do any good to speak up.

"Listen, if you have a complaint, there are proper channels you can go through. But I honestly don't see the problem." Gus straightened up and gestured for Nikki to come up to the counter.

John stepped back in front of it before she could and pointed his finger straight at Gus.

"You are absolutely clueless! You have no idea how lazy these cops are! Half the time I see them sitting around eating instead of patrolling the streets. The other half they're harassing the tax-paying citizens of this town by handing out nuisance traffic tickets. If there was any actual police work done around here, I think I'd die of shock. You'll see, Marlo's murder will go unsolved, just another crime to add to the pile that these officers and detectives are too lazy to investigate."

Nikki bit into her bottom lip and held her breath. She thought of how hard Quinn worked to solve the crimes that happened in Dahlia. Often, she didn't see him for days because he wouldn't take a break until a crime was solved.

"All right, John." Gus looked from Nikki to John, his cheeks bright red. "That's enough. I have other customers to help."

"Yeah, you enjoy that, because with the way this town is going downhill, you won't have any customers left to serve." John barely looked at Nikki as he turned and stormed out of the store.

Nikki noticed the thick coat he wore and the heavy boots on his feet. He looked prepared for a snowstorm. She wondered if he treated everything in life as an impending disaster.

"I'm so sorry about that, Nikki." Gus continued to blush as he began to ring up her items.

"It's all right, Gus." Nikki smiled. "Everyone is entitled to their opinion."

"Maybe, but sometimes I wish we could put a muzzle on certain people." Gus rolled his eyes.

Bruno gave a faint whimper.

"Oh, he's not talking about you." Nikki gave the dog a light pat. "He seems extra riled up, or is he always like this? I don't think I know him."

"Ever since he retired, he's been storming around town complaining about one thing or another." Gus shook his head. "Marlo's murder has him all twisted up." He paused and looked up at her. "I heard you had something to do with that."

"Marlo's murder?" Nikki's eyes widened as she wondered if Scott had been spreading accusations against her because of the dogs chasing him.

"I mean, that you were in the area when they found the body." Gus winced.

"I was." Nikki nodded, then sighed. "And just so you know, Quinn is working hard on solving it. I'm sure he will find the killer."

"I'm sure he will, too. Don't let anything John says get to you. I think the man has watched one too many crime movies. He seems to think he knows what's best in any situation. I hope he finds a hobby soon, maybe it will help him to relax." Gus accepted her payment and handed her the change. "Thank you for coming in, Nikki. Happy holidays."

"Happy holidays to you too, Gus." Nikki smiled at him, then looped the bag over her wrist. As she led the dogs back out onto the sidewalk, she tried to shake off John's comments about the police. As Gus had implied, he likely was just a lonely, old man with nothing better to do than complain.

Nikki led the dogs down the sidewalk in the direction of Marlo's Butcher Shoppe. As she approached it, she noticed a car parked in front of it. Her eyes shifted from the car, to the front window of the shop. A chill carried through her as she noticed the neon open sign. Could Carolyn really have opened up so soon after her brother's murder?

Nikki started towards the shop, but a crowd on the other side of the street caught her attention. A group of protesters paraded back and forth in front of Chop Chop Butcher Shop. It had been running huge sales and incentives in an attempt to steal Marlo's business. Nikki had avoided shopping there mainly because it was part of a big chain, and she preferred to support local businesses. Now, it seemed that Chop Chop had the full attention of the animal rights' protesters that had been targeting local butcher shops and dairy farms.

Nikki recognized one of the men in the group. He was young and slender. He held his sign higher than all of the others. When he glanced in her direction, she noticed the dark circle that surrounded his eye and part of the bridge of his nose. Yes, it was the same person. She frowned as she walked across the street in his direction.

"A fellow animal lover." He smiled as he crouched down to greet the dogs.

"Yes, I do love animals." Nikki braced herself for the barrage of insults she expected. She'd been walking to Marlo's shop the week before, when the protesters had surrounded it. Upon seeing her heading for the door, they had hurled slogans and warnings at her. Marlo burst out of his shop and told them to leave. When they refused, he'd landed a solid blow on this man's face.

"They are beauties." He looked up at her, his eyes narrowed. "How can you take such good care of these dogs but not care how animals are treated in places like that?" He pointed to Marlo's shop.

"I do care." Nikki pursed her lips as she watched him rise to his full height. At almost a full-foot taller, he seemed to loom over her. "But we all have different ways of showing it."

"Sure, it's always safer to keep your opinions to yourself." He raised an eyebrow. "I suppose that's why you didn't have a word to say when the police arrived last week? Yes, that's right, I remember you. I'm Adam by the way."

"I told the officer what happened, Adam." Nikki looked into his eyes.

"You did? Because they seemed pretty convinced that I was the one who initiated the attack." Adam offered a mild shrug. "I have no idea how they could have gotten that idea."

"I was scared, and Marlo reacted to that. He was trying to protect me." Nikki tightened her grip on the leashes to make sure the dogs didn't stray too far from her. "It is frightening when you surround a person and shout at them."

"But I didn't put my hands on you, did I?" Adam shook his head. "Or that horrible man. But I'm still the bad guy." He looked across the street at Marlo's shop. "He had it coming." He shifted his attention back to her, his lips drawn into a tight, thin line.

"Is that what you think?" Nikki asked. "That he deserved to be murdered?"

"I think we get what we give. It's karma." Adam raised his eyebrows, his clear blue eyes sparked with a hint of animosity. "It's not for me to decide who lives or dies, now is it?"

Adam's last words hung in the air between them. Nikki could barely take a breath as she wondered if he had decided it was up to him. Had he decided to take karma into his own hands? Perhaps he wanted to get revenge on Marlo because he had punched him in the middle of a crowd of his fellow protesters.

"Maybe Marlo was a butcher, but are you a murderer?" Nikki muttered as she guided the dogs away from him.

cold breeze ruffled Nikki's wavy, shoulder length hair as she crossed the street towards Marlo's Butcher Shoppe.

Nikki focused on the bright neon open sign in the window of the shop. Had someone made a mistake and turned the sign in the window on?

She hurried the dogs up to the door and grabbed the handle to open it. She expected it to be locked, but instead it swung open freely.

"Hello?" Nikki called out into the empty space. With her nerves on edge, she searched for an explanation for the shop being open. Clean, white tiles covered the floor and most of the walls of the shop. A large, front counter with a wide, glass display window stretched from one side of the shop to the other. A swinging half-door allowed entry between the front of the shop and the rear of the shop. An open doorway led to the rear of the shop, where meat was prepared for sale and extra supplies were stored.

"Hello? Is anybody here?" Nikki's heart pounded. Why was the shop open if no one was there? Wasn't this how Gavin had described the scene from the day before.

"Hello?" Nikki pushed the door open farther. "Is anyone here?"

Nikki held her breath as she was about to step inside.

"Can I help you?" Carolyn stepped out through the door that led to the back.

Nikki took a sharp breath the moment she saw her.

"Carolyn, what's going on? Did you know that the open sign is on and the door is unlocked?"

"Please keep the dogs outside." Carolyn narrowed her eyes. "And yes, I know. I opened the shop up this morning. The police are finished here, it's no longer a crime scene, so I was free to open it for business. Everything has been cleared out or cleaned, but we just got a new delivery today and we have orders to fill."

"But—" Nikki took another sharp breath.

"You think it's too soon?" Carolyn shrugged. "You're not the only one, trust me. But deliveries still need to be made, and there are many things that have to be taken care of here. I would love to sit at home and grieve, but that's just not an option right now."

"Of course." Nikki cleared her throat, she didn't want to offend the woman, but she couldn't comprehend how she had opened the business up so soon. If her own brother had been killed, she doubted that she would be able to do anything other than search for his killer. "I wanted to reach out to you, to see how you are, but I didn't have your number, and I'm not sure where you live."

"Yes, I try to keep to myself." Carolyn walked around the counter and joined her near the front door. "I really don't want anyone checking on me. I don't know how to handle the onslaught of niceties. People ask me how I am, and if I told them, I know that they wouldn't want to be near me. But if I lie, then I'm the one betraying myself and my brother, aren't I?" She shook her head. "It's a very difficult thing to deal with. I know people mean well, but I can't stand it. At least Betty is helping out as much as she can, but she is really only available for a few hours a week. But at least the business can keep going, at least for a little while."

"I imagine it must be overwhelming trying to deal with all of this." Nikki nodded at the thought. "No one can understand exactly what you're going through right now."

"That's right. But they can certainly judge me for opening up the shop. I have received some strange looks so far today." Carolyn looked past her at a person who lingered in the doorway, then continued to walk by. "It's not that I'm a cold person, Nikki, or that I didn't love my brother. When you experience certain things in life, you learn that it doesn't really matter how you feel, life continues on whether you like it or not, whether you want it to stop or not."

"I understand." Nikki frowned, then looked into Carolyn's eyes. "I just wish you didn't have to deal with it. Isn't there someone that could help? Didn't Marlo work for another butcher before he opened his business? Maybe his old boss could take over for a little while so you wouldn't have to do all this."

"Philip?" Carolyn gave a short laugh, then shook her head. "The last thing he wants to do is help me, trust me. In fact, he's part of the reason that I had to make sure we opened up today. Between him and that ridiculous shop across the street, they're like sharks circling, just waiting to snap up all of the customers we lose because of Marlo's death. And I can't." She took a sharp breath, then narrowed her eyes. "I can't let them win. I can't let them profit from my brother's death." She tipped her head towards the group of protesters. "And I won't let them think they have shut us down. For all I know any of these people could have had something to do with my brother's murder, and I'm not going to stand by and watch them dance on his grave."

"I see your point." Nikki's mind spun with a mixture of emotions. She could feel the determination in Carolyn's words, she understood the woman's passion to protect her brother's business and memory, but it still seemed impossible for her to be so well functioning. "I'm sorry to have interrupted. I was walking past and I saw the sign so I wanted to check that everything was okay. Everything was so chaotic yesterday."

"Nikki, you have no idea how grateful I am to you." Carolyn filled the door frame as she gazed at her. "If you hadn't come when you did, who knows what would have happened between Gavin and Scott. You were a huge support to me yesterday."

"Well." Nikki glanced over at the noisy

protesters then looked back at Carolyn. "I wish I could have done something to help."

"You did help, a lot. The support you offered me yesterday means a lot to me." Carolyn sighed as her cell phone rang. "Sorry, it's non-stop around here right now."

"I'll let you get back to it." Nikki started down the sidewalk. She glanced back over her shoulder as she heard the door of the shop close. She couldn't help but wonder who would be making demands of Carolyn the day after her brother, the owner of the shop, had died. Why would she feel so pressured? Wouldn't most people understand if their orders were late?

Nikki dropped the dogs off at Petra's house, then hurried in the direction of Sonia's house. She had promised to attend the tasting with her at the hotel. When she arrived at her home, Sonia met her in the driveway.

"I hope you don't mind, I already took Princess for her walk so that we can get an early start. There's so much to do." Sonia sighed. "I always think these parties are a good idea when I start, then I wonder why I ever got myself into it."

"It's going to be great." Nikki gave Princess a quick kiss on the top of her head. After Sonia locked up, Nikki followed her to her car. On the drive to the hotel, Nikki filled her in about her conversation with Carolyn, and Adam.

"How unnerving." Sonia frowned. "You shouldn't go near him, not alone, Nikki. He seems off."

"You may be right about that." Nikki shook her head. "It gave me the chills when he started talking about karma. His eyes, they were just so cold."

Sonia parked in front of the hotel and stepped out of the car.

"I can understand passion for protecting animals, I certainly support that, but it sounds like his passion is more about causing trouble."

"How much is the question?" Nikki mumbled as they neared the door of the hotel. As much as she wanted to debate the possibility of Adam's involvement, she knew that this party was important to Sonia, and she wanted to be supportive.

"Let's eat." Nikki winked at Sonia.

CHAPTER 8

"I'm glad that you decided to come with me today." Sonia stepped through the door of the hotel.

"Me too." Nikki smiled as she followed after her. "Good company and food. What could be better than that?"

"I couldn't agree more. Although it would be nice if Princess could join us." Sonia draped her arm around Nikki's shoulders and led her towards the main ballroom in the hotel. "Everything is set up in here, and they have already started decorating for the party. I do hope that it will be a success. I've decided to add a fundraiser to support Carolyn as well. It can help with the funeral costs."

"That's so thoughtful of you, Sonia." Nikki smiled at her as they stepped into the ballroom. "I'm sure that she will be so grateful for it." Her mind flashed back to the fierceness in Carolyn's eyes as she demanded that Quinn do his job. She could understand that she was grieving her brother and wanted justice.

"So, did you know about this dinner that Quinn planned?" Nikki raised an eyebrow as she looked over at Sonia.

"Oh, he finally told you, huh?" Sonia grinned. "I think it's a wonderful idea, and I'm honored that he thought to include me."

"Of course, you would be included." Nikki looked from the Christmas tree in the corner to the tinsel draped across the ballroom's high ceiling. "Wow, they are really putting a lot of effort in."

"Hey John!" A man called from the top of a ladder leaned against one of the walls. "Can you hand me some green tinsel?"

Nikki looked at the man at the base of the ladder. From his gray, bushy beard she recognized him as the same man that she'd seen in the hardware store.

"Sure, I can." John walked over to some tinsel.

"No, green please, I already have the red." The man on the ladder called out.

"Sorry, you'll have to point the green tinsel out to me. I'm colorblind." John shook his head. "I can't tell the green from the red."

"No problem. It's on the table over there. By the candles." The man on the top of the ladder pointed to a pile of green tinsel on one of the tables.

"Do you know John, Sonia?" Nikki looked over at her.

"John Winter. Not well. I've seen him over the years around town, but this is the first time I've met him properly. He volunteered to help decorate, along with a lot of other people. It's so nice that so many people in town are working to help get this party together." Sonia took a sharp breath. "Sometimes I wonder if it will ever happen, though. It seems like there's so much to do to be ready."

"Don't worry, I'm sure you'll pull it off." Nikki nudged her with her elbow. "You are famous for being able to pull anything off."

"I'm not sure if that's a good thing, or a bad thing." Sonia laughed as she led Nikki to a large table in the center of the room. "So, the assortment of foods are all possibilities for the menu, I'm just not sure which ones will be best. I have a hard time making a decision when it comes to food, because people have such different tastes. That's why I'm so glad that you're here to help."

"I'm happy to be here. I am good at eating." Nikki sat down in one of the chairs. Her mind wandered instantly back to Marlo. He supplied many of the local businesses. "Do you think Marlo supplied the meat to this hotel?" She glanced at Sonia.

"I'm sure he did. Actually, I saw one of the delivery vans at the hotel the day before yesterday. I was here to make some choices about the tablecloths and cutlery, and I noticed the van heading back to the delivery dock. I was glad to see it, actually. I knew at least I could count on the quality of the meat." Sonia sighed. "I wonder what will happen to Marlo's shop now?"

"I guess it will close. I doubt anyone would buy it and keep it open when there is so much competition." Nikki frowned. "I'm sure Nathan will be happy that there won't be competition directly across the road from him anymore."

"I'm sure he will be, too." Sonia narrowed her eyes. "That place wouldn't have a chance to make it if Marlo was still in business."

"Probably not." Nikki sighed as she turned her attention to the trays being brought to the table.

"Excuse me, Mrs. Whitter?" John stepped up beside the table.

"Yes?" Sonia looked over at him.

"Are there any special requests you have for the decorations?" John asked.

"No, it all looks great. Thank you." Sonia smiled.

"Okay, I'm going to step out for a few minutes. My son, Dale, works here and he's asked for my help with a delivery. I'll be back shortly to finish up." John smiled at her, then looked past her and smiled at Nikki.

"No problem, John. I appreciate all of your help." Sonia gave him a light pat on the arm. "Do whatever you need to help your son."

"Thank you." John turned and walked out of the ballroom.

Nikki watched him go, her brows knitted.

"What is it?" Sonia gave her a light nudge with her shoulder.

"I don't know. I heard him talking to Gus at the hardware store about how bad the police force is in this town, and how they should do more to solve crimes. I guess it kind of rubbed me up the wrong way." Nikki shrugged and picked up a fork. "Shall we dig in?"

"Absolutely." Sonia grinned as she picked up her fork as well. "We both know there's nothing wrong with the Dahlia police force. Don't let him get to you." She rolled her eyes. "Everyone has an opinion."

"So true." Nikki dug her fork into the risotto placed in front of her. Although she hadn't eaten much, she still didn't have much of an appetite. She moved the rice around her plate for a few moments, then put a forkful in her mouth. As she savored the well-seasoned mouthful, she forgot everything else for just a moment. Then the real world came crashing in, literally, as some of the tinsel that had been strung along the ceiling landed on the top of her head.

"Oops!" Sonia laughed as she helped get the tinsel off her head. "It's crazy around here."

"But the food is great." Nikki grinned as she dug in.

By the time they finished the tasting, Nikki was full.

"Any ideas for the menu?" Nikki looked over at Sonia. "I wasn't much help, it all tasted so good, I couldn't choose."

"I know, maybe I should get all of it." Sonia patted her stomach and laughed. "I think I've got a few favorites. It's a pity you can't make the party because you are volunteering at the shelter that day, but at least you got to try some of the food." She stood up from the table. "Let's get out of the way and let them finish the decorating. We can sort out the food selection while we walk."

"Good idea." Nikki nodded. She caught a glimpse of John as he entered the ballroom again, with a younger man at his side. He looked to be about her age, perhaps a little older. He wore the uniform of the hotel and seemed to be engrossed in conversation with John.

"Is that John's son?" Nikki nodded her head towards the younger man.

"It must be. I spoke to him earlier in the week. He was moving some of the decorations into the room. Dale, I think his name is." Sonia glanced at Nikki. "Did you want to meet him?"

"No, I'd rather stay as far away from John as possible." Nikki did her best not to glare.

"Oh, look at you, so festive." Sonia laughed as she pointed out a few shreds of tinsel in her hair. "Don't forget, it's the holidays." She met Nikki's eyes. "It's okay to have a little fun."

"Who can have fun when this town is overrun with criminals?" John shot a glare in their direction.

"Thanks for this. It really was a good distraction." Nikki laughed and ignored John's comment as she pulled the tinsel from her hair.

"I'm glad." Sonia wrapped her arm around Nikki's and shot a look of warning at John. Then she turned her attention back to Nikki. "Now, what's next?"

"I'm going to pick up Rocky and Bruno for their afternoon walk. Do you want to join me?" Nikki smiled as she sensed that Sonia wanted to spend time with her.

"I'd love to. That way you can fill me in on all of the details." Sonia winked at her then led her out through the door. "The dogs aren't in trouble, are they?"

"No, Quinn made sure that Scott didn't make a complaint." Nikki's eyes landed on a delivery van from Marlo's as it pulled around to the front of the hotel. "Wow, Carolyn wasn't kidding about them being busy today." She frowned. "Is that Scott in the driver's seat?"

"It sure looks like him." Sonia nodded as she watched the van drive by. "I'm surprised he's back to work."

"I know." Nikki raised an eyebrow. "It shocked me to find out that Carolyn had the shop back open so quickly, and now to see that Scott is already making deliveries after the drama that unfolded just yesterday."

"It sounds like she's a business woman first." Sonia shrugged as she pulled open the door to the car. "I'm sure they had deliveries they were due to make, and a supply of meat already ordered. She may just be trying to make whatever money she can from the business before she shuts it down."

"That's true, she mentioned as much when I spoke to her. It's possible that the business wasn't even profitable, with all of the competition they were facing." Nikki settled in the car. "Why don't you drop me off and I'll pick up Rocky and Bruno, and you can go get Princess. I'll meet you in town. Maybe we can see if the protesters are there and we can speak to them. We can't eliminate them as suspects at the moment."

"Okay, I'll meet you there." Sonia nodded, then pulled out of the parking lot of the hotel.

"You know that guy John?" Nikki narrowed her eyes. "He really seems a little off."

"Don't worry, I'll keep my eye on him." Sonia

turned down the road that led to the residential area of Dahlia.

Nikki began to fill Sonia in on the details she'd discovered about the crime so far, and the information that Quinn shared with her.

"He's right that it might not have been premeditated, but I tend to lean more towards what you're saying. I still think it's very possible that Marlo was targeted because he was alone, and someone knew that no one was going to be there with him. So, who would know that Pam had been called away?" Sonia turned down a side street.

"I've been thinking about that. My guess is that when the daycare called, Pam called Ethel to see if she would cover her. Knowing Ethel's personality, I'd guess that she might have declined to come in, or not answered her phone at all." Nikki tapped her fingertips against her knee. "But that would mean that she knew that Pam was leaving."

"Also, whoever called her from the daycare." Sonia frowned. "Maybe someone was there that overheard the call. Or maybe Marlo even told someone else himself. Maybe he complained to someone? Scott?"

"According to Scott he saw Marlo in the

morning when the shop opened, and then not again until he was dead. So, I don't think that he would have known about Pam being called away." Nikki shook her head. "And even if he did, he had so many deliveries to make that morning. Why would he have chosen that morning to kill Marlo?"

"Pam said her daughter was sick, right?" Sonia pulled up in front of the house and stopped. "What if she had something to do with the murder? What if she made up the story about her daughter being sick and having to be picked up from daycare? Maybe she and the killer made a plan together to use the opportunity when Marlo would be alone, to kill him?"

"Maybe." Nikki frowned as she considered the idea. "She doesn't strike me as a murderer, but she is handling a lot on her own. Maybe she did it for money? Or maybe Marlo had threatened to fire her, and she was afraid to lose her job?" She shook her head. "No, that wouldn't make sense, because with Marlo dead I'm sure the shop will be closing down, so she will lose her job anyway."

"I'm not sure, but I think it's worth digging into." Sonia tipped her head towards Petra's house. "Looks like the boys are waiting for you."

Nikki laughed as she spotted the two dogs in the window.

"Yes, it does. All right, I'll meet you in town." Nikki hopped out of the car.

"See you soon." Sonia waved to her as she pulled away.

CHAPTER 9

*N*ikki gathered the dogs and headed towards the center of town. As she walked, she tried to sort out what she and Sonia had discussed. No matter how she twisted things she couldn't see Pam as a killer, but maybe that was because she took an instant liking to her. Ethel on the other hand, the thought that she might have killed Marlo seemed to fit. But why? As far as she knew she had no motive to commit the crime. She needed to find out more about Ethel and her relationship with Marlo.

As Nikki neared the center of town, she spotted the delivery van from Marlo's again. It was parked outside a restaurant, with its rear doors open.

Nikki glanced around and didn't see anyone nearby.

"It won't hurt to take a look will it, pups?" Nikki guided the dogs towards the van. She wondered if perhaps the GPS in the van had a record of the vehicle's movements the day before. If so, maybe she could prove whether Scott was lying about where he had been all morning. She guessed that Quinn had already checked, but it didn't hurt to double-check just in case. He had so many things to handle. As she neared the van, the two dogs began to pull hard in the direction of the back of it. Nikki held tightly to them, but the smell of the meat seemed to intoxicate them.

Bruno began to growl as he tugged at the leash.

"You two must be hungry." Nikki rolled her eyes as she pulled them back.

A quick peek into the van revealed rows of boxes on rolling shelves. She could see that some of the boxes were green, and some were red. All of the meat in the boxes looked the same, so she guessed the colors were random.

Rocky gave a sharp bark and tried to climb up into the back of the van.

"No!" Nikki tugged Rocky back just as Scott walked out through the side door of the restaurant.

"Hey! What are you doing back there!" Scott shouted at Nikki. "Get those dogs away from there and keep them away from me!"

"I'm so sorry, Scott, I was actually looking for you." Nikki's heart raced as she clung to the leashes. "I just wanted to apologize for yesterday, it was all so chaotic."

"Oh?" Scott glared at her. "So, you don't think I'm a murderer?"

"No, of course not." Nikki shook her head and shortened the leashes to make sure the dogs stayed right beside her. They seemed more interested in the van than they were in Scott, but she couldn't risk them antagonizing him again. "It's just that I was shocked when you barreled into me and they were confused, maybe frightened, I think. They saw you, and overreacted. I'm so sorry about that."

Nikki thought that he should apologize for running into her, but she didn't want to cause any trouble.

"Yeah, well, it was a shock to see Marlo like that." Scott shoved his hands into his pockets as he looked at the dogs. "Maybe they chased me because they really like the smell of the meat, huh?"

"Yes, I think they do." Nikki frowned.

"That's probably why they went after me yesterday." Scott rubbed the sleeve of his shirt.

"I'm very sorry about that. They're very mild mannered most of the time. I appreciate you not filing a complaint." Nikki met his eyes. "It was my fault, I was shocked when you ran into me and then Gavin was shouting at you, and I'm sure they picked up on that."

"But you're okay now, are you?" Scott gazed back at her, his dark eyes insistent.

"Of course." Nikki smiled.

"You need to keep these dogs away from me, and my van, got it?" Scott slammed the doors on the back of the van shut.

"Scott, are you sure you're okay to be working after such a shock? I'm surprised that Carolyn opened the shop up so fast." Nikki stepped in front of him as he headed for the front of the van.

"The deliveries have to be made." Scott met her eyes again. "Now, get out of my way."

A shiver crept up Nikki's spine as she noticed the change in his tone. The implied threat made her wonder if Gavin had been right to suspect him in the first place.

"I really am sorry about what happened yesterday." Nikki's heart slammed against her chest.

"If it happens again, you'll be more than sorry."

The moment Sonia set eyes on Scott, she detected his animosity. His tightened shoulders, narrowed eyes, and stern tone set her nerves on edge.

Princess gave a sharp bark as Sonia led her down the sidewalk in Nikki's direction.

"What's going on here?" Sonia looked straight into Scott's eyes. "Nikki, is he giving you a hard time?"

"Just having a discussion." Scott shrugged as he looked past Nikki, back into Sonia's eyes. "You have a problem with that?"

"I do." Sonia stepped up beside Nikki.

"It's all right." Nikki took a deep breath and stepped aside. "Scott needs to get on with his deliveries."

"I bet." Sonia glared at him as she pointed to the van. "You know the way I'm guessing?" She draped an arm around Nikki's shoulders.

Scott shook his head, then climbed into the driver's seat of the van.

Sonia felt Nikki's shoulders tense under her arm.

"It's okay. I'm right here."

Nikki looked over at her and smiled a little.

"I could have handled it."

"I know you could have, but it never hurts to have some backup." Sonia watched as the van pulled out into the street. "What was that all about? Was he threatening you?"

"Not in so many words, but yes." Nikki shook her head. "This day just gets crazier and crazier."

"It does." Sonia looked down in time to see Princess and the two other dogs greeting each other. "They seem to be doing well."

"Yes, but I shouldn't have taken a chance with them being near Scott. I think the smell of the meat on him just drives them crazy." Nikki frowned.

"I think they just smell that he's not a nice person." Sonia quirked an eyebrow. "But I guess they are the only ones that know what they are smelling. I'm sorry it took me a little longer than I intended to get here. I stopped by Ethel's to speak with her."

"You did?" Nikki turned to face her. "Did you find anything out?"

"Only that she doesn't like people showing up at her front door, or Chihuahuas." Sonia grimaced as she scooped Princess up into her arms. "I think it's time we took a deeper look at who in this town had a grudge against Marlo."

"That sounds like a good idea, but it leaves us a pretty big suspect pool." Nikki tipped her head to the side. "I think we need to find out more about Marlo. I don't think that Carolyn will tell me anything more about him and maybe there are things she doesn't know about him. But there are other ways to learn more."

"What do you mean?" Sonia took a step closer to her.

"I can't get into Marlo's shop because it's open, and if Carolyn catches me sneaking around in there, she won't let it go easily." Nikki pursed her lips.

"Then where do you plan to look?" Sonia frowned.

"I thought maybe we could go see if we can find out anything at his apartment building. I doubt we'll be able to get into his apartment and I doubt that the police left anything relevant there, but we can maybe see if there are any neighbors around that we can ask about him. Carolyn apparently lives with him, but if she's at the shop she's not at his apartment." Nikki looked into her eyes. "It's not far from here. Three streets over." She started down the sidewalk.

Sonia put Princess down on the sidewalk. Immediately, the tiny dog marched over to Rocky and Bruno. She stood nose to nose with them for a few seconds, then began to lead the way.

Sonia smiled to herself at the sight of her bold dog. She knew that if Rocky and Bruno had a problem with her, they would have no problem overtaking the much smaller dog, but apparently Princess didn't know that, or didn't sense any animosity from them.

"Are you sure about this, Nikki?" Sonia asked. "Quinn wouldn't like it if he found out you were investigating."

"I'm sure, I want to do this. It's not too far ahead." Nikki tipped her head in the direction of a nearby apartment building. "Apartment 106, it's on the first floor." She paused as they neared the entrance. "You should stay here, I'll let you know what I find out."

"Have you lost your mind?" Sonia chuckled, and shook her head. "There's no way you're going up there by yourself. We'll be right there with you."

"Sonia." Nikki frowned and met her eyes. "What if the police catch us snooping around?"

"Nope, I'm not taking no for an answer." Sonia looked straight back at Nikki. "Now let's hurry, before the next wave of traffic shows up." She pointed to oncoming traffic behind them.

"All right, quickly." Nikki sighed as she led the two German Shepherds across the street and through the gates of the apartment complex. She glanced back and pointed Sonia in the direction of the apartment. The apartment looked locked up tight, but she noticed a maintenance man at the end of the hallway.

"You wait here with the dogs and I'll go see if I can find out anything." Sonia winked at Nikki, then walked up to the man. "Excuse me, sir, do you have a minute to help me, please?"

The man turned to face her. His cheeks were covered with a thin beard, and his eyes hooded by thick eyebrows. His eyes narrowed as he looked at her.

"Sure. What can I do for you?" He smiled slightly.

"I wanted to speak to Marlo in apartment 106, but I can't get hold of him." Sonia gestured towards the apartment. His face tensed as he turned to look at the apartment.

"Do you know him well?"

"No, not really, just from his shop."

"Well, I'm sorry to say Marlo passed away."

"What? Oh no, that's terrible." Sonia feigned shock.

"He was a nice guy."

"Oh, I'm so sorry for your loss." Sonia shook her head. She looked over her shoulder to see Nikki following behind, casually, as if she had no idea who Sonia was.

"Thank you." The man nodded.

"What happened?" Sonia asked.

"I can't give out that information." The maintenance man shook his head. "Sorry I can't be more helpful, but I have to go." He looked at his watch.

"I understand." Sonia smiled at him although she wished he would give her some information.

The man walked down the hallway and Sonia turned, then hurried in Nikki's direction. She was almost to her, when a scream caused her to stop in her tracks.

CHAPTER 10

or a split second, Nikki wondered if that scream had come from her. The entire world felt disjointed, as if she had somehow slipped into another version of it. Then her mind snapped back to reality. It wasn't her that screamed, but someone not far away.

"What was that?" Nikki spun around to face Sonia as her heart raced.

"I have no idea, but it came from over there." Sonia pointed to the next parking lot over from the apartment complex. The plaza had several small shops in it and a large department store for its anchor.

"I don't see anything strange." Nikki hurried

towards the gates of the apartment complex. "We should go see what it is. It sounded so awful."

"I think we're too late." Sonia tilted her head towards an assortment of emergency vehicles that flew past them in the direction of the parking lot.

Nikki's heart dropped as she wondered who the sirens were for. She quickened her pace towards the parking lot and followed after the emergency vehicles. When she neared the center of the commotion, her stomach lurched at the sight of a familiar van. It belonged to Marlo's Butcher Shoppe.

"Sonia?" Nikki turned back to look at her.

"I see it." Sonia took her hand and squeezed it. "It could just be a coincidence."

"No, I don't think so." Nikki peered around the side of the ambulance and caught sight of the victim on the ground several feet away from the van. She couldn't quite see who it was.

"Nikki." One of the officers walked up to her. "What are you doing here?"

Nikki met his eyes and recognized him as Jim, one of the rookies that Quinn often spoke about.

"I heard the scream." Nikki pressed her hand against her chest as she looked at him. "What's happened?"

"It's not good." Jim shook his head. "It looks like a hit-and-run."

Nikki noticed the flurry of movement around the victim suddenly ceased.

Her heart sank.

"Who is it, Jim?" Nikki held her breath as she waited for his answer.

"It's Scott." Jim cleared his throat. "The delivery driver from Marlo's." He narrowed his eyes. "Nikki, I don't think you should be here. You should really go." He looked past her, at Sonia.

Nikki could barely take a breath as she tried to fathom how it could be Scott.

"Ma'am?" Jim met Sonia's eyes. "You should really take her away from here, please."

"What's the problem?" Sonia wrapped her arm around Nikki's shoulders. "We're not causing any harm."

Jim frowned, glanced over his shoulder at the victim, then looked back at the pair.

"He didn't make it. This is a police investigation now. I just think it would be best if Nikki wasn't here."

"An investigation?" Nikki's eyes widened. "A homicide? You think someone killed him on purpose?"

"I'm not the detective. It could have just been a random hit-and-run. Either way it's a crime scene." Jim glanced towards the entrance of the parking lot. "The detective will be here any second, you should go, it's not going to look good for you to be here. Are you listening to me?"

"Right, yes." Nikki took a step back.

"Why wouldn't it look good for her?" Sonia's eyes narrowed. "She has as much right as anyone else to be here."

"Yes, she does. But with her being involved at the other crime scene—" Jim's voice trailed off, then he cleared his throat.

"He's right." Nikki took a slow breath as she recalled Scott's accusations against her. They'd had a disagreement over the dogs and now he was dead, too. How would that look? "We should go, Sonia." Nikki walked in the direction of the apartment complex.

"We should go home, Nikki." Sonia tried to meet her eyes.

"No." Nikki shook her head, then glanced back over her shoulder. "No, not home. I want to see if I can find out more. Let's just get out of sight for the moment."

"Nikki, I'm not sure that's a good idea." Sonia

frowned as she looked back at the gathering of police vehicles. "Whatever is going on, we know two things. First, Quinn is going to have an entirely new investigation on his hands. Second, whoever killed Scott, and likely whoever killed Marlo, is still on the loose."

"That's the thing." Nikki leaned back against the fence that surrounded the apartment complex and closed her eyes. "I was so certain that it was him, then I was certain it wasn't, Sonia. I don't even know what to think now. Was it just some random coincidence?"

"I don't think that's possible." Sonia leaned against the fence as well. "Is life ever that random?"

"It can be, but it's unlikely." Nikki frowned. "There has to be something here. Something that we're missing." She ducked her head as she spotted Quinn on the scene.

Seconds later she heard quick footsteps heading in her direction.

"Nikki?" Quinn paused in front of her. "What are you doing here?"

"We were out walking the dogs." Sonia shrugged. "We heard a scream."

"Quinn, it's terrible. How could someone have killed Scott, too?" Nikki asked.

"We don't know what this is just yet. All of the evidence on scene indicates it was likely a hit-and-run. Someone didn't see Scott step out around the van, maybe they were a little distracted or drunk, and they hit him." Quinn pursed his lips.

"That's what you're going with?" Nikki looked into his eyes. "Really?"

"It's what I'm starting with." Quinn put his hand on her shoulder as he stared back at her. "Step by step, I'm going to find out what happened here."

"What if whoever killed Marlo is after more than just him, more than just Scott. What if there are more targets on the killer's list?" Nikki straightened up.

"I can't just jump to conclusions. I can't just assume that the same person who killed Marlo killed Scott, even if it is the easiest leap to make. I will find out the truth, but not by letting my judgment get clouded." Quinn looked over at Sonia. "Please make sure Nikki goes home. I'll be there as soon as I can."

"I will." Sonia nodded as she wrapped her arm around Nikki's shoulders.

"I can't believe this." Nikki sighed as she watched him walk off. "I can't believe that he's going to work this like a random hit-and-run. I can't believe that he can't see that it must be connected."

"He has to do things by the book, Nikki." Sonia squeezed her shoulder. "Just try to be patient."

"How can I be patient? Who might be next? Carolyn? Pam? Ethel? Betty?" Nikki pressed her hand against her forehead and shook her head. "None of this makes sense. All I know for sure is that I can't do nothing. I need to help find out who did this."

"Yes, we do." Sonia sighed. "Yes, we do."

Startled by the entire event, Sonia stayed close to Nikki as they walked away from the scene. She tried to put together in her mind the how and the why of Scott's death, but nothing added up.

"Do you think someone did this because of what happened to Marlo?" Sonia looked over at Nikki.

"I have no idea." Nikki frowned. "But you heard what that officer said. He didn't think I should be around the crime scene. Me being at the scene of two homicides in as many days doesn't look very good, does it?"

"Don't worry about that." Sonia patted her shoulder. "You've done nothing wrong."

"Maybe not, but Scott just threatened me not

even an hour ago. How do you think that's going to look?" Nikki sighed as she looked down at the dogs that remained close to her side as she walked.

"No one has to know about that." Sonia narrowed her eyes.

"What if someone saw us, though?" Nikki shook her head. "Oh, this is just awful. How can this be happening? First Marlo, and now Scott?"

"It is terrible." Sonia squeezed her shoulder then looked towards the apartment complex. "I'm sorry that I couldn't get any information from the maintenance man."

"That's all right." Nikki shook her head. "I don't know where to look next, now that Scott is no longer a possibility."

"Well, that's not exactly true." Sonia paused at the entrance of the apartment complex and then continued walking. "Just because he was killed, that doesn't mean that he isn't the one who killed Marlo. In fact, maybe he was killed because of that."

"Then someone must know that he was the murderer." Nikki frowned. "If they know that, then why wouldn't they have turned him in?"

"That's a very good question. Maybe they didn't have proof? Maybe they were worried that it would incriminate themselves?" Sonia scrunched up her nose. "Something smells fishy about this entire situation. I think there's a lot more going on here than meets the eye." Sonia picked up Princess and followed behind Nikki as they walked in the direction of Sonia's car. As she heard sirens wail in the distance, her stomach flipped. It was too late for Scott, but maybe they could find something that would lead them not only to Marlo's killer, but Scott's as well.

"It appears so. But what, is the question?" Nikki smiled as they approached her friend, Gina's café.

"How about some tea?" Sonia offered. "Something to relax your nerves."

"Good idea." They all crossed the road to the café.

Nikki often took the dogs she walked to the café. Gina always made sure there were water bowls for her customers' dogs set up outside.

"Is this okay?" Sonia chose one of the two empty tables available. It was a table for four away from the other tables that had customers at them. They sat down in the chairs as the dogs happily took turns drinking from the water bowl. Princess went first and the other two waited patiently. Nikki and Sonia smiled at the sight. Once they were finished drinking, the two German Shepherds lay down on the floor at Nikki and Sonia's feet, while Princess jumped into Sonia's lap.

The door to the café swung open and Gina stepped outside with an order book in her hand.

"Hi ladies." Gina smiled. "And pups." She turned towards the dogs.

"Hi Gina." Nikki admired how Gina always looked so cheerful and welcoming. "How is everything?"

"Busy." Gina nodded. "Which is good. Looks like you've been busy, too. I heard that you were involved with the commotion at the butcher shop. Poor Marlo. I heard you got knocked over. You weren't hurt, were you?"

"No, I'm okay." Nikki smiled.

"You'll have to tell me all about it, when I have some free time." Gina's eyes lit up. "You must try my candy cane cupcakes."

"Absolutely!" Nikki and Sonia replied in unison, then laughed.

They had just finished placing their orders when Nikki noticed that Sonia looked past her towards someone behind her.

"Hi Billy." Gina waved in the direction that Sonia was looking in and Nikki turned to see why the man had Sonia's attention. It was the maintenance man from Marlo's apartment complex.

"Gina." He smiled.

"There aren't any seats inside, sorry." Gina shook her head. "The book club has taken over the majority of the tables." She turned to the only empty table outside. "You can take—" She stopped mid-sentence as a couple sat down at it.

"You can join us." Sonia smiled. "There's enough room."

Billy eyed the dogs then looked from Nikki back to Sonia.

"Aren't you the ladies from the apartment complex?"

"We are." Sonia smiled brightly as if she had nothing to hide.

"Well, don't mind if I do, thanks." Billy sat down at the empty seat farthest away from the dogs.

"I'll get your usual." Gina smiled sadly. "I'm sorry about what happened to Marlo, Billy."

"Me too." Billy frowned. "He was such a great guy."

"He was a good guy." Gina nodded then walked back into the café.

"I'm sorry, I didn't realize you were close to

119

Marlo." Sonia looked at Billy. "Did you know him for long?"

"No, not at all, only a few months." Billy smiled. "We met when his hot water system broke and I had it fixed. He was so young."

"Oh, it's a great loss." Sonia nodded.

"He had some grand plans." Billy's shoulders slumped.

"He did?" Nikki asked.

"Yes." Billy leaned back as Gina delivered their orders. After thanking her he continued. "He was keeping them hush hush, but I guess it doesn't matter now. He was planning on launching a new range of smoked meat. He wanted to keep it a secret to keep the competition at bay. At least for a while. He was so excited about it. He had every right to be, it was so good."

"You tasted it?" Sonia sipped her tea.

"Yes, I let him set up a shed behind my house for smoking the meat, and in exchange he gave me free meat and even taught me how to smoke it." Billy smiled. "I don't know what I'll do with the shed now." He took a bite of his cupcake.

"Sounds like a great deal." Nikki leaned forward with interest. "Do the police know about the shed?"

"Nope. I need to tell them." Billy shook his head.

"I've had a couple of days off, so the police haven't caught up with me, yet." He looked at his watch. "I better get going."

"Do you think we could look at the shed?" Nikki asked. "Before the police tear through it. I would love to see how a meat-smoking shed works." She smiled with false enthusiasm.

"I don't see why not, but you'll have to look from a distance." Billy finished off his coffee. "I don't want anyone inside until the police have searched it."

"Of course." Sonia nodded.

"It's on Winder Way." Billy smiled. "I have to go past my mother's house to drop something off, but it's about a twenty minute walk, so I'll meet you there."

"Okay, thanks." Sonia smiled.

Billy left some cash on the table, popped the last of his cupcake into his mouth and hurried down the street.

Sonia and Nikki quickly finished their cupcakes. The peppermint from the candy canes was delicious and they were too good to leave behind. When they were finished, they left cash and a tip for their meal. Then they grabbed the dogs' leashes and headed towards Winder Way.

"Well, that was interesting." Nikki smiled. "But I don't expect to find any evidence in a meat-smoking shed."

"Me either." Sonia led the way. "But we definitely won't find anything if we don't try."

"You read my mind."

CHAPTER 11

On the walk to Winder Way, Nikki's mind spun as she recalled the way Jim looked at her. Yes, it wasn't going to be easy to explain how she happened to be at two crime scenes. She guessed there had been a few people that overheard her confrontations with Scott.

By the time they reached Winder Way, the dogs were well walked but were still full of energy.

"We didn't get a house number. How are we going to know which property the shed is on?" Nikki asked.

"There it is." Sonia pointed down the side of a house.

"Good spotting."

They waved to Billy who stood next to the shed.

Nikki, Sonia and the dogs walked briskly towards it.

"I'll stay here with Rocky and Bruno." Nikki stopped a few feet away from the shed.

"I don't have long." Billy took a key out of his pocket and opened the door.

Nikki's stomach flipped. How would Quinn react if he found out that she and Sonia had landed up at Marlo's shed.

Sonia looked into the shed and went to take a step inside.

"Sorry, you can just look. You can't go inside." Billy's phone rang. "I have to take this." He stepped to the side out of earshot but watched Sonia closely.

Sonia had hoped that he would let her have a look around inside. She knew she couldn't sneak inside with him watching. She discreetly reached into her purse and pulled out a piece of gum. She popped it into her mouth and tucked the wrapper into her pocket. She peeked inside the shed. From what she could see everything looked neat and in its place.

Billy ended the call and started to walk over to them.

"Sorry, I have to go." He called out. "I have to pick up my son from baseball practice."

As Sonia turned around, she let Princess jump down from her arms. The dog dodged back towards the shed, and Sonia scooped her up just as she was about to go through the door. As she cradled the Chihuahua in one arm, she scooped the gum from her mouth and placed it and its wrapper into the latch of the door just before Billy reached them.

He pulled the door to the shed closed.

"Thank you for showing us." Sonia called out to Billy as she walked towards Nikki. "Sorry, I didn't get to see much," she said to Nikki when they were out of earshot.

"Well, at least you tried. I doubt there was much to see." Nikki shrugged.

Sonia waved to Billy as he drove past them down the street.

"I did try. But I also made sure we had a way in." Sonia met her eyes as a faint smile settled on her lips. "So, do you want to have another look? Now might be a good time, I'm sure the police are still focused on what's happening in the plaza with Scott."

"True. But how are we going to get in?" Nikki asked.

Sonia started towards the shed. "We'll just walk right through the door."

"Isn't it locked?" Nikki hurried to catch up with her.

"I still have a few tricks up my sleeve." Sonia winked and tried the handle of the door. It didn't budge. She gave it a firm push, and the door popped open. "If you block the latch, it doesn't matter if it's locked." She smiled as she held the door open for Nikki. "I'll go have a look around, you better stay out here with the dogs."

"Okay." Nikki nodded as she stood outside the doorway and poked her head in to look around.

There was a smoker in the middle of the shed. In the corner there were a few papers piled up. They appeared to be old newspapers and some papers that had two columns that listed usernames and passwords. Sonia snapped some pictures of them as she sorted through them. One piece caught her attention. It appeared to be a handwritten letter, though it wasn't signed. As she read over the contents, her heart pounded.

If you don't stop your illegal activities, I will kill you.

Sonia stepped away from the paperwork knowing the police would find the papers once they knew about the shed.

She snapped a picture of it and showed it to

Nikki who still stood by the door holding the dogs' leashes.

"Wow, that's interesting." Nikki nodded as she looked at Sonia's phone.

Sonia walked back to the papers. They were resting on a small table with a tablecloth over it. She lifted the corner of the tablecloth back and peered underneath. She gasped and stumbled back as she clung tighter to Princess.

"What is it?" Nikki stepped forward holding the dogs' leashes tightly and lifted the corner of the tablecloth. She peered through the glass of a container. The movement took her breath away. "Roaches!" The container was filled with roaches.

"It seems to me that Marlo had some very unhealthy and unscrupulous habits." Sonia grimaced. Her heart raced as she began to realize that maybe Marlo wasn't so innocent after all. "My guess is that he did exactly what Philip claimed he did and planted those roaches in his shop and products and left bad reviews on social media."

"I hate to think it, but I don't know of any other explanation." Nikki sighed and snapped a picture of the container.

"There's nothing else here." Sonia headed

towards the door. "We should head back. We'll have to tell Quinn about this place."

If Billy caught them in the shed, she was not sure what he would do but it would probably mean big trouble and could cause a lot of problems for her and Nikki, especially Nikki, if it was reported to the police and Quinn found out.

"Nikki? We should get going." Sonia carried Princess as she stepped outside. Nikki and the dogs followed after her. Sonia removed the gum and closed the door to the shed behind them.

Sonia, Nikki and the dogs walked back towards the center of Dahlia. On the way they discussed the best way to let Quinn know about the shed without getting themselves into trouble. In the end they decided that there was no way around it they would just have to tell him about the shed and what they had found. They couldn't risk waiting for Billy to tell the police and the potential evidence possibly disappearing.

"I'd better get these pups back home." Nikki patted the German Shepherds on their heads.

"All right, I think I'm going to speak to Philip now that we think that Marlo really did plant the roaches in his business. Maybe he'll tell me something."

"Good idea." Nikki nodded. "I'll come with you."

"No, that's okay. It might be better if there's just one of us. You've already spoken to him about Marlo. When he sees you, he might be on the defensive straight away." Sonia shrugged. "What do you think?"

"Yes, you're probably right." Nikki smiled slightly. "But I think his shop will be closed already."

Sonia looked at her watch.

"You're right. I didn't realize it was so late." She smiled. "I'll speak to him in the morning. I'll see how I go with Philip and then I might try speak to Nathan as well."

"Okay." Nikki nodded. "Keep me updated."

"I will." Sonia gave her a quick wave, then led Princess towards her car.

Nikki headed back in the direction of Rocky and Bruno's temporary home. When she reached it, she checked to make sure the dogs had plenty of food and water. Then she stepped back out through the door. As she did, she almost bumped into Quinn.

"Quinn?" Nikki's eyes widened.

"Nikki, I think we need to talk." Quinn gestured to his car.

"You hunted me down?" Nikki raised an eyebrow.

"I took a chance that you'd be here, I knew you had the dogs with you. You're not answering your phone." Quinn led her down the sidewalk towards his car.

"Oh, I must have left it on silent." Nikki pulled her phone out and noted several missed calls from him. "Sorry. Is something wrong?"

"No nothing. I had to leave you abruptly at the scene after what happened to Scott and I wanted to chat with you." Quinn smiled. "Do you have a minute?"

"Sure."

They walked to his car.

"It turns out that it looks like Philip was telling the truth." Quinn looked over at her. "We found records of fake social media accounts on Marlo's computer. They were the accounts with posts that made complaints against Philip's shop. Claiming there were roaches in the food."

"Really?" Nikki's heart raced. Did he mention it because he already knew that she and Sonia had been in Marlo's shed?

"Yes." Quinn drove in the direction of his house. "And what's even more interesting is that we found bags of cash hidden under the floorboards in Marlo's apartment."

"You did?" Nikki's mouth fell open.

"Yes, it looks like he might have been involved in something underhand." Quinn glanced over at her.

"I might have some information for you." Nikki winced slightly.

"You do?"

"I do." Nikki explained about the meat-smoking shed and what they had found.

"Well, it turns out that my guys are on the way over there now. We managed to get hold of Billy just before." Quinn's eyes fixed to the windshield as he turned onto his street.

"Oh, that's good." Nikki nodded. "There are certainly some interesting things to find there."

Quinn parked the car in his driveway, then stepped out.

Nikki followed him onto the porch. He let Spots out and he ran straight over to Nikki, his tail wagging.

"I missed you, too." She bent down to greet him and rubbed behind his ear. Even though it was cold, Nikki and Quinn sat on the porch swing, their favorite spot, with Spots lying on top of both of them. Their coats on and a blanket over their legs with Spots keeping them warm. Nikki stroked Spots' head and instantly felt herself relax.

"Like I said, we found thousands of dollars in Marlo's apartment." Quinn looked over at her, his expression stern. "That's why I've been looking into Marlo's finances." His eyes narrowed. "He is in a lot of debt and his business was doing terribly, it was losing a lot of money. But over the last few weeks business seems to have turned around. It keeps getting better and better. We also found the social media accounts." His phone beeped with a text and he picked it up to look at it, then continued. "Now, the roaches confirm that it's pretty clear that Marlo did exactly what Philip accused him of doing. Which certainly makes Philip a suspect."

"What do you think about the finances, though?" Nikki settled her head against his shoulder and closed her eyes. "I heard that Carolyn is supposed to be in charge of marketing and helping to increase business. Maybe business has improved because of her."

"Maybe." Quinn settled his chin on the top of her head. "According to our financial analyst, the business is improving even though he's still in a lot of debt, which isn't surprising because Nathan said that Marlo had got most of the business only recently. I have to go out to Marlo's shed. But I want to sit here with you for a few minutes first."

"I hope this is solved soon." Nikki sighed and rested her head on the crook of his shoulder. She smiled as he wrapped his arms around her. "I wish we could stay here forever."

"Me too," Quinn whispered as he tipped his lips down to kiss the top of her head.

"You don't actually think that what happened to Scott was a random hit-and-run, do you?"

"I have to investigate it that way until I find some evidence that proves it wasn't." Quinn frowned. "Having a biased opinion when looking at a new crime is a good way to turn it into a cold case. I need a clean slate while I gather the initial evidence."

"You have to go. Don't you?"

"I do. I wish I didn't have to go to work. We could be snuggled on the couch, instead of out here in the freezing cold." Quinn laughed.

"I'm not cold." Nikki grinned as she nestled closer to him. "I'm nice and warm."

"Good." Quinn tightened his arms around her. "I hope this is all solved before the holidays, but I don't like the chances."

"You still have a little time." Nikki sighed as she

recalled how many things she still hadn't gotten done. "Have a little faith, it's the season of miracles, remember?"

"It feels more like the season of murders." Quinn cringed at the thought.

"No more." Nikki leaned up to kiss his cheek. "You're going to get all of this figured out, and then we're going to have a blissful Christmas." She tipped her head from side to side. "Well, maybe not blissful. But we'll try."

"Why not blissful?" Quinn grinned as he looked into her eyes.

"Let's just say, I'm expecting a few fireworks and awkward moments." Nikki took a deep breath. "Getting the families together is a big step."

"Too big?" Quinn's eyes narrowed.

"No." Nikki smiled as she settled her head against his chest. "It's just right."

CHAPTER 12

The following morning, after Princess had been for her morning walk and she had everything she needed, Sonia looked up the phone number for Meat Stop. She placed an order and gave her credit card information over the phone. She would have a reason to see Philip, if she was a paying customer.

Armed with the knowledge of what they had found in Marlo's shed, she drove in the direction of Philip's shop. It was pretty clear to her now, that Philip hadn't made any wild accusations against Marlo. Instead he had tried to tell the truth. She parked in front of the shop and stepped inside to find a bit of a crowd around the front counter. She lingered near the door and listened to bits and pieces of conversations between Philip and his customers. As she did, she recognized a voice. She ran her gaze across the gathered customers and within moments picked out a familiar face.

"Ethel?" Sonia smiled as she met the woman's eyes.

"Sonia?" Ethel took a slight step back from the counter. "What are you doing here?"

"I've placed an order. Now that Marlo's will be closing soon, I have to find a new shop to order from." Sonia raised an eyebrow as she looked over at Ethel. "What are you doing here?"

"Marlo's isn't closing." Ethel crossed her arms. "Not if Carolyn has anything to do with it."

"Oh?" Sonia frowned. "But Betty can only do a few hours a week. Do you think Carolyn will hire someone new?"

"She already has to hire a new driver." Ethel rolled her eyes. "I knew that Scott was trouble from the beginning."

Sonia's eyes widened at her words. How could she talk so dismissively about someone who had just been killed?

"What made you think that?" Sonia held back any additional words. She hoped the woman would continue to talk, if she didn't push her too hard.

"The way he looked at Carolyn for one. And the way that Carolyn looked back at him for two." Ethel shook her head. "The two of them couldn't keep their paws off each other."

"What?" Sonia took a sharp breath. "Are you saying they were in a relationship?"

"I'm not officially saying anything, just like they didn't officially say anything, but sure I caught them cuddled up in the walk-in sometimes and rocking the van now and then." Ethel shrugged. "It happens, I know, but if Marlo had ever found out he would have been furious."

"Why is that?" Sonia ignored all of the other sounds around her as she focused only on Ethel's words.

"He was weirdly overprotective of Carolyn. He even warned Scott to stay away from his sister, and that if he ever found out that he made any advances, he would pay the price." Ethel winced. "I guess that Marlo can't protect her any longer."

"Too bad she wasn't more protective of him." Sonia shook her head. "Maybe he would still be here."

"Oh, that's not her fault." Ethel sighed. "I don't know who killed Marlo, but if Carolyn had been there, she would have protected him. Anyway, I'm just here to get a good glimpse of the competition. Carolyn says we will be back at work after the holidays."

"I see." Sonia tilted her head to the side. "So, you're not upset at all that Marlo was killed, and now Scott was, too?"

"What?" Ethel lifted her eyebrows. "What did you just say?"

"Scott was killed, too. A car hit him yesterday. You didn't know?" Sonia's heart skipped a beat as she hadn't expected to break the news to Ethel.

"I had no idea."

"I'm surprised that Carolyn is so eager to stay open with all that's going on." Sonia noticed the shock etched into Ethel's features.

"I have to go." Ethel pushed her way past Sonia, and soon the other customers in the shop did the same. Sonia found herself face to face with Philip.

"How can I help you?" Philip smiled at her.

"Hi Philip." Sonia set her hands on the counter. "I'm here to pick up my order, and I wanted to ask you a few questions as well."

"You do?" Philip's eyes narrowed. "If they're about the specials they are listed there." He pointed to the chalkboard on the wall.

"They aren't." Sonia didn't break eye contact with him. "Marlo used to work here right?"

"He did." Philip narrowed his eyes. "And?"

"And, you two were quite close. Weren't you?" Sonia kept her tone even and determined.

"At one point, yes." Philip sighed.

"So, what happened? Did you turn him down for a raise? Did you say something to offend him, or was it the other way around?" Sonia tipped her head to the side. "Something made him so angry that he wanted revenge."

"I hired my nephew. I had to let Marlo go. I told him it would just be temporary, but he lost it." Philip shrugged. "I would have hired him back within a month, but not after what he did."

"He set your business up. He left bad reviews, planted roaches in your food and let them loose in your shop so that you would fail the inspection, after he called to make a complaint." Sonia glanced around at the counter, and the floor beyond it. "You keep a pristine shop. There's no way you had a problem with bugs here."

"I don't know, and I can't prove it." Philip held up his hands. "So, why should I even bother thinking about it?"

"But you did, didn't you?" Sonia looked back at

him. "I mean how could you not think about it. I bet since that day the bad reviews went up and your reputation was tarnished, you've done nothing but think about it. I see the way you have your arm around Marlo in that picture. He was more than an employee to you, wasn't he? Maybe Marlo found a father figure in you? Maybe you were more like family?"

"It doesn't matter." Philip's tone sharpened. "It's water under the bridge, as they say."

"Maybe it is, now." Sonia nodded.

"Look, I don't know what you're thinking but I had nothing to do with Marlo's death." Phillip scowled. "I cared about him."

"I'm sure you did." Sonia smiled. "Did you still care about him even after he ruined your business?"

"He didn't ruin anything." Philip pointed around him. "Business is thriving."

"I can see it is. You must take pride in your business, offer a good product." Sonia stared straight into his eyes. "What Marlo did must have made you angry."

"I don't like what you're suggesting. I cared about Marlo." Philip slapped his hand hard against the counter.

"I'm not suggesting anything. I'm sorry if you feel like I am." Sonia grimaced.

"Yeah right." Phillip slapped the counter again. "I know what you are implying."

"That's quite a temper you have there, Philip." Sonia kept her voice calm.

"You don't know me." Philip leaned across the counter, his eyes hard as they locked to hers. "You don't know anything about my temper. I would never have hurt Marlo." He pointed towards the door. "Get out!"

Sonia backed away then, as his voice shook with rage. She thought about asking for her order but decided against it. The money wasn't completely wasted, as she had managed to see Philip's reaction to her questions, even though it didn't end well. She couldn't help but notice the way his face filled with passion when he spoke. Why was he so angry? Was it because he was guilty? Or offended that he might be suspected of murdering Marlo?

CHAPTER 13

Sonia settled in her car and gripped the steering wheel tight. She could still feel the tremble in her hands. She knew that Philip might not react well to her questions, but the intensity of his reaction had taken her by surprise. He'd become so very angry, and although he had hit the counter, he hadn't lifted a finger in her direction. He certainly had motive to kill Marlo, but had he done it? She sent Nikki a text asking her to meet at her house, then started her car. As she drove home, she thought about the possibility that Philip killed Marlo. However, her thoughts shifted back to Ethel in the crowd of customers. She claimed to be there to check out the competition, but Sonia wondered if that was just a cover and she was working with Philip to get rid of Marlo.

Sonia parked in her driveway just as Nikki walked up the sidewalk towards the house. She waved to her as she stepped out of her car.

"I'm so glad you're here." She led her up to the front door.

"You said it was important, something about Philip?" Nikki followed her through the door. After she gave Princess a cuddle, they walked to the dining room table and Nikki sank down into one of the chairs.

"You should have seen him, Nikki, he was irate." Sonia shook her head. "It wasn't what he did, it was how he did it. I don't know, I just don't think he killed Marlo. I think he cared about him."

"That's fine, but not thinking he did it, doesn't eliminate him as a suspect." Nikki tapped her fingertips against her knee. "We know that it's likely that Marlo left false reviews and did infest his shop with roaches, so Philip certainly does have plenty of motive, but that doesn't mean that he would go to all the trouble of killing him. I mean it is a bit extreme. If he wanted revenge, he could have simply called in complaints against him, and at some point Marlo's business would have suffered. I think you're right, I think we might be barking up the wrong tree with him. But we have to keep him in mind for now. So, we're down to a few possibilities. We have Adam, Nathan, and maybe Philip."

"And Ethel." Sonia narrowed her eyes. "She was at Philip's shop when I arrived. She claimed to be there to spy, but something felt off. She seemed shocked and a little worried when she saw me there." She shook her head. "I can't quite put my finger on it, but something just left me ruffled. But maybe it's just her personality." She took a breath. "Oh, and Scott, don't forget Scott. We haven't been able to clear him as a suspect." She frowned as she looked over the list on her phone. "Nothing that we've found has made it impossible for him or Gavin to be the killer. Quinn said that the timing didn't add up, but maybe someone was covering for them. Quinn seemed to think that Gavin's alibi seems to be completely airtight compared to Scott's."

"Let's think about that." Nikki closed her eyes and tried to put together Scott's last moments. "If it wasn't a random hit-and-run, if Scott was targeted, then whoever killed him had to know where he would be at the time of the delivery. Ethel, as an employee of the shop, would probably know his route, right?"

"Yes, she would, or Pam?" Sonia nodded as she added a note on her phone.

"If this was a targeted killing, then to me, there are two possibilities of why." Nikki opened her eyes and sat forward in her chair. "Either, someone believed that Scott killed Marlo, and they killed him to get revenge, or both Scott and Marlo knew about something that someone else would kill to keep quiet."

"Interesting." Sonia narrowed her eyes. "What do you think that could be?"

"I'm not sure, but maybe it has something to do with the money in Marlo's apartment. Where was the cash coming from?"

"Maybe Marlo was desperate because he was losing so much money that he got involved in something illegal and that got him killed. Maybe Scott witnessed the murder, and he was too scared to tell the police, but the murderer killed him to keep him quiet."

"Maybe." Nikki sighed. "Ethel said that Scott and Carolyn were in a relationship. I would like to talk to Carolyn about it. If it's true and not just a rumor maybe she knew Scott well and has a clue as to what was going on with him. Or what might have led to his murder."

"Maybe, but we'll have to broach the subject sensitively." Sonia nodded. "I doubt she would want the fact that she was in a relationship with Scott getting around."

"I know. Hopefully, she will give us some information that might finally lead to the murders being solved." Nikki sighed. "I feel like we only add more suspects, we haven't been able to rule anyone out. Except for maybe Philip."

"Maybe I can help with that." Sonia tapped her fingertip against her chin. "You talk to Carolyn, and I'll see what else I can find out about our collection of suspects."

"Hold that thought." Nikki snatched up the phone as it started to ring. "Quinn? Oh, did he?" She frowned as she looked at Sonia. "I'm sure. Yes, anything you can do would be helpful." She ended the call, then met Sonia's eyes. "For once it's not me that's in trouble. Philip called in a complaint about you."

"Seriously?" Sonia grimaced. "I feel like I had more to complain about since he's the one who lost his temper."

"Maybe, but as of now, Quinn would like you to

steer clear of Philip's shop. Okay?" Nikki held her gaze.

"Okay, no problem. He's not going to arrest me, is he?" Sonia laughed.

"No." Nikki smiled as she picked up her purse and headed towards the door. "I'm going to see if I can catch Carolyn while she's still at the shop. I think she has more chance of talking to me there." She reached down to give Princess a pet and a cuddle, then looked up at Sonia. "I'll let you know what I find out."

"Good. Princess and I are going to go out for a bit, too." Sonia scooped her up. "I want to go to the pet store and see if I can get something festive for Princess to wear at the party. Then I'm going to see what I can find out about the other suspects."

"Just stay away from Philip, okay? Even if you don't think he's a murderer, I don't like the way that he talked to you." Nikki opened the door, then looked back at Sonia.

"I promise." Sonia held up one hand and smiled. "I'll stay away from Philip."

Nikki stood outside the shop and watched Carolyn

through the window for a few minutes. She tried to decide whether she should go ahead and reveal that she knew about Carolyn's relationship with Scott. She didn't know if it was true, and she also didn't know how Carolyn would react if she brought it up. When she finally pulled the door open to enter the shop, Carolyn spun around to face her.

"I'm sorry to bother you." Nikki paused in front of the counter and met her eyes. "I know how busy you must be."

"It's no bother, just tell me what you need." Carolyn looked straight back at Nikki.

"I just wanted to see if you were okay. I know that you have so much on your shoulders and now with Scott's death, I can only imagine how you're feeling. How are you handling that?"

"Is that what you're here for?" Carolyn narrowed her eyes. "To ask me about my emotional well-being?"

"That, and I'd still like to pick up my order of bones if that's possible. Christmas is right around the corner, and I would like to make sure I have something special as a treat for my boyfriend's dog."

"I see." Carolyn smiled. "I'll ask Betty to bring them out." She popped her head into the back then stepped back behind the counter. "Betty will bring them out in a minute. I wrapped them up for you this morning. Grant was going to deliver them, but since you're here, I can just give them to you."

"Grant?" Nikki leaned against the counter and smiled.

"The new driver." Carolyn nodded. "A friend of mine."

"You hired a new driver already?" Nikki's eyebrows raised. "That must have been such a difficult task for you, while dealing with the shock of Marlo and Scott's deaths."

"Business doesn't stop for grief. It just doesn't. I can't even explain to you how insane all of this is, and how much I am pushing through it, but no matter what I do the orders still have to go out, they have to be filled, the meat still has to be sold before it goes bad. Once things calm down and I get a full-time butcher, maybe I can take a breath or a break. But for now, I'm focused on what needs to get done. So, when someone comes in here and asks me, no matter how well meaning they are, how I'm handling all of this, you can only imagine what it does to me. I can't stop myself from being in the middle of this chaos, but at least while I'm working, I can forget, just for a little while. But when someone reminds me, I lose it." Carolyn took a shaky breath. "I can't focus, I can't think, and I'm ready to crumble."

"I'm so sorry." Nikki frowned. "I didn't mean to cause you any of that pain."

"I know that. And, it's not your fault. I've refused to have Pam or Ethel back until after the holiday, because they can't compartmentalize like I can. Pam gets weepy and they both start talking about things that I can't think about. So for now, it's just me, Betty and Grant, and we will find a way to get through this."

"I admire your strength, Carolyn." Nikki smiled.

"Thank you. I have to get back to it." Carolyn started to turn around.

"How much do I owe you?" Nikki pulled her wallet out of her purse.

"It's on the house." Carolyn smiled slightly. "When I found out about my brother you were there to help me. For that, I am grateful. This is just a small way that I can show that."

"Thank you." Nikki smiled. "I know that Quinn is doing his very best to find out what happened to Marlo. I hope he can figure it out before the holiday."

"That would be nice." Carolyn's shoulders relaxed.

"Carolyn, I'm sorry to ask you this, but I've heard some rumors. Is it true that you and Scott were together?" Nikki locked her eyes to the other woman's.

Carolyn didn't react. She didn't tear up. Instead she spoke in an even tone.

"Let me guess, you heard that from Ethel?" Carolyn rolled her eyes. "She always has her nose in everyone's business. Scott and I worked together. We might have had a little fun here and there, but it was nothing serious." She shrugged. "Like I said, business is about business." She sighed. "I really do have to get back to it." She walked towards the preparation area. "Betty won't be long."

A few seconds later a woman who looked to be in her thirties stepped out of the back. She wore a hairnet and a white apron. Nikki recognized her as Betty. She had met her a few times.

"Here you go, Nikki." Betty held out the package.

"Thanks Betty." Nikki was about to ask her a question when the phone in the shop rang.

"Sorry, I have to get that." Betty sighed as she turned towards the phone.

Nikki still wanted to ask her some questions.

She pretended to look at the food in the display case as Betty answered the phone.

"You've been told not to call here until things calm down." Betty barked into the phone. "It will be handled, that's all you need to know."

The tone in Betty's voice surprised Nikki. She had heard the woman be stern, but this was something far different. She sounded almost ruthless. She continued to look in the display case, while Betty's voice continued to escalate.

"You don't have to know the how and the why. You'll have your stuff. That's been made perfectly clear enough times. There's no reason that you should be questioning me. If you continue, then the whole deal will be called off. Don't think it won't!" Betty slammed the phone down in the cradle.

Nikki jumped at the sharp sound. Her shoe scuffed against the floor.

"You're still here?" Betty spun around to face Nikki.

"Oh yes, sorry, I was just looking at some of the meat." Nikki took a step back from the counter.

"Oh, I didn't realize. I thought that you had left." Betty scowled as she looked at Nikki. "Sorry that you had to hear that."

"It sounded pretty serious." Nikki narrowed her

eyes as she studied her. "Is there something going on? Is someone giving you a hard time?"

"It's just business." Betty waved her hand. "With everything going on, a lot of our regular clients are threatening to pull out. Carolyn has explained why some of the deliveries are late, but not everyone can be courteous. Carolyn has said that I need to make it clear that if they don't want to work with her, then they can take their business somewhere else."

"I think you made that clear." Nikki smiled some. "It just sounded so intense. I know that people can get upset over late deliveries, but are you sure that's all that was about?"

"I'm sure." Betty glanced up at the clock. "Now, I really have to get some things done. Just call in an order to Carolyn if you'd like something else, all right?"

"Yes, I will. Thanks." Nikki's feet remained locked to the floor as Betty walked through the door to the back. Nikki had no intention of leaving. Not until she found out who Betty was speaking to on the phone. There was only one way she could think of to find out. She held her breath for a few seconds and listened to the movements in the back.

When Nikki felt certain that Betty had stepped farther towards the back of the preparation area, she stepped around the counter and hurried over to the phone. She did her best to keep her movements soundless as she picked up the phone. She pressed the redial button, then waited as the phone began to ring. With each ring, her heart pounded faster. At any second Carolyn or Betty could walk back out to the front, or a customer could walk into the shop and raise the alarm about Nikki being behind the counter.

Finally, the line picked up.

"What?"

Nikki cleared her throat. She looked towards the door that led to the back. Then she whispered.

"The deal is still on, right?"

"Betty?" The man snapped. "What kind of game are you playing with me? If I don't get me my shipment, I'm going to tell Wolf to use someone else. You don't want to mess with Wolf."

Nikki hung the phone up quickly. She hurried around the counter and straight out through the door of the shop. Her thoughts spun with the memory of the man's tone and threatening words. Wolf. She doubted that the delivery he was talking about had anything to do with meat. Betty was definitely involved in something, but what exactly?

CHAPTER 14

*A*lthough Sonia did her best to stay out of any kind of political issues, she was aware of the protests that had been happening throughout town, and also in the surrounding towns. She could understand and respect their right to speak up against what they considered to be cruelty. But she felt that their tactics could cross the line at times. Murder certainly crossed the line.

It wasn't hard to keep track of their movements as they took to social media, and traditional media, to rally their troops. When she walked towards the local pet store, she spotted a group of protesters outside Chop Chop Butcher Shop, armed with signs and their voices. As they chanted, she heard the passion in their voices. It took her back to a different time, a time when the entire country was filled with people who had something to fight for. She paused for a few moments, just to observe, then she led Princess forward, towards the man she'd hoped would be there.

"Adam?" Sonia stepped up beside him.

"Yes?" Adam turned to look at her and lowered his sign. "Oh, look at this little angel." He cooed as he bent down to greet Princess. "She's just the cutest thing that I have ever seen. May I pet her?"

"Of course." Sonia smiled as she watched the man stroke Princess' fur. If he was a murderer, he was one with good taste. While he continued to pet the dog, she turned her attention to the tattoo on his shoulder. "Isn't that interesting, what is it?"

"It's a Japanese symbol. It means, all life is sacred." Adam straightened up and looked into her eyes. "I got it to honor the animals."

"I see." Sonia eyed the redness around the edges of the tattoo. "It looks fairly new."

"It is." Adam smiled as he glanced at the tattoo. "It's my alibi."

"Excuse me?" Sonia raised an eyebrow.

"Don't think I don't know why you're sniffing around here. I've seen you with Nikki. And, I've already been cleared by the police. I was at the tattoo parlor up the street at the time of the murder. Both the artist and his camera verified it." Adam shrugged. "I believe all life is sacred. I would never justify taking a life, even if it was the life of a monster."

"Marlo wasn't a monster." Sonia narrowed her eyes.

"Maybe not to you." Adam gave the tattoo a light tap. "But to me, he was." He raised his sign in the air again. "Protect all life!" He shouted as he turned to join the rest of the crowd.

Sonia scooped Princess up and sighed. She hadn't expected such a strong reaction from him, but his alibi sounded airtight. She made a note on her phone, then continued on to the pet store, as she walked past Chop Chop she noticed security cameras outside the shop. Maybe they had filmed something on the day of the murder? She decided that as soon as she finished at the pet store, she would take Princess home and go visit Nathan at Chop Chop.

When Sonia stepped inside Chop Chop Butcher

Shop, she noticed a few customers at the counter. She lingered near the lunch meat display and eyed the prices. The woman behind the counter spoke in a kind tone to the customers.

"It's been so crazy around here. I know it's hard to keep up with the holiday cheer with everything going on. That's why we're giving all of our customers a gift card along with their purchase, just to put joy back into the season."

Sonia guessed that it was the best marketing scheme they had ever come up with. While the shop across the street dealt with two murders, Chop Chop stood to make a nice profit, and could afford to extend the goodwill to its customers. As the other customers began to clear out, Sonia edged closer to the register. She could hear voices in the back of the shop. She guessed that one of them belonged to Nathan, the manager of the shop.

"Can I help you?" The young lady, Donna, according to her name tag, smiled at Sonia.

"Actually, I'd like to speak to your manager if possible." Sonia smiled in return.

"Is there a problem?" Donna's smile faded some.

"No problem. I just want a chance to speak with Nathan." Sonia hardened her tone just enough to ensure that the cashier knew she couldn't be easily ignored.

"Sure, I'll see if he's free." Donna poked her head into the back. "Nathan? There's someone out here that wants to see you."

"Yes?" Nathan stepped into the front of the shop.

"Hi Nathan." Sonia extended her hand to him. "I'm Sonia Whitter."

"Mrs. Whitter, I've heard so many wonderful things about you." Nathan shook her hand. "Did you need some help with that gala you're throwing? It's short notice, but I'm sure we can provide whatever you need."

"No, actually the hotel is catering the event, and I believe they get their supply from Marlo's." Sonia tipped her head towards the front window.

"Yes, most of the restaurants in Dahlia and the surrounding towns order from there." Nathan sighed. "I'm not sure why, but for the last few weeks they preferred to work with Marlo, even when I undercut him."

"It won't be a problem anymore." Sonia sighed.

"Oh yes, terrible what happened there." Nathan frowned. "It doesn't surprise me, though, with what was going on over there."

"What do you mean?" Sonia narrowed her eyes.

"There were some suspicious guys going in and out of that place after hours." Nathan sighed. "I tried talking to Marlo about it, but he acted like I was crazy."

"Suspicious guys?" Sonia shook her head. "Like who?"

"I don't know them personally, some of them I've seen in town working at the bars and restaurants and some aren't from around here, I can tell you that much. And they always showed up after closing. I don't think Marlo was working on those days. It was whenever Betty was working, but I can't say for sure." Nathan studied her. "What is it that you needed?"

"I wondered if you had some video footage of the sidewalk in front of your shop, at the time that Marlo was killed?" Sonia met his eyes.

"The police already asked. Unfortunately, our camera wasn't working that day. One of the protesters broke it." Nathan glared through the front window at them. "I had to go three towns over that morning to get a new one."

"Oh? So, you weren't here when Marlo was killed?" Sonia searched his expression for any dishonesty.

"Mrs. Whitter, it surprises me that you're so interested in something so dark." Nathan crossed his arms. "What is this really about?"

"I care about Dahlia, very much, and I don't want a murderer to run free on its streets. It puts all of us at risk. Don't you think?" Sonia forced a small smile to her lips.

"I suppose so. Lucky, I have an alibi. I gave my receipt to the police to prove my whereabouts, and they have me on camera at the store buying the new camera." Nathan narrowed his eyes. "I returned to Dahlia shortly after Marlo's body was found."

"Oh, I just wanted to check if you could offer any more information as to who might have done this." Sonia smiled.

"I can't." Nathan shook his head. Sonia could see him tense at the question.

"Perhaps not you, maybe one of your employees?" Sonia looked at the young girl who still stood near the register.

"Not a chance. She doesn't know anything about this." Nathan's voice rose slightly. He appeared to be getting angry.

"Okay, I'm sorry to have bothered you." Sonia nodded. "I would like to get some meat, please." She always made Princess home-cooked meals and she was running out of ingredients.

"Okay." As Nathan put her order together, she wondered if he had started to get angry with her questions because he was offended, or because she'd stepped just a little too close to the truth.

Armed with the new information about Betty, Nikki headed straight for the police station. If she could catch Quinn at his desk, then she had a better chance of getting the information to him. She waved to a few of the officers as she headed back to his office. Through the open door she caught sight of him, his body tense, his lips drawn into a tight line. She knew that look. He was hyper-focused and determined. Which meant he likely still didn't have much of a lead. She hoped that she could change that.

"Do you have a minute?" Nikki tipped her head against the doorway and watched as he shuffled some papers on his desk.

"I'd love to say yes, but the truth is, no." Quinn looked up at her. "I'm sorry, I've just stumbled across something from the paperwork from the shop that I need to follow up on."

"What is it?" Nikki raised an eyebrow as she tried to peer at the papers on his desk.

"I can't tell you." Quinn met her eyes. "At least, not yet. I want to make sure that my theory is solid."

"Maybe I could help?" Nikki's heartbeat quickened as her curiosity increased.

"No." Quinn looked straight into her eyes. "Not this time. I have to hurry." He brushed past her, pausing long enough to kiss her cheek. "I'll check in with you soon."

"Okay, be careful." Nikki fought the urge to catch his hand. Something about his tone left her uneasy.

Nikki looked at the pile of papers on Quinn's desk. She knew she should just leave, but curiosity had been something she couldn't avoid since she was a young child. If she was curious about something, she couldn't let it go, until she was satisfied. It had led to many obsessions, and quite a few adventures. She couldn't help but take a quick peek. The paper on top was a call record for Marlo's Butcher Shoppe. She quickly took a few pictures of it on her phone.

"Detective?" An officer poked his head through the door.

Nikki took a sharp breath as she looked up at the officer.

"Hi Jim."

"Hi." Jim stared at her. "Sorry, I was just looking for Quinn."

"Oh, you just missed him. He was in such a rush, and he seemed a little stressed. I just thought I'd help him straighten things up a bit." Nikki's heart raced as she wondered if he would believe her.

"Oh okay. Yes, this case has us all running around like crazy." Jim shook his head. "It's usually so quiet around here, it's hard to believe that all of this could happen."

"Yes, it is." Nikki slipped her phone into her pocket. "I should get going. I'm sure if you give Quinn a call, he'll get back to you."

"Yeah, I'll try that." Jim stepped aside so that she could pass by.

"Actually, Jim, do you think that you could do me a favor?" Nikki met his eyes as she lingered in the hallway not far from him.

"What kind of favor?" Jim eyed her with a half-smile. "Something that's going to make Quinn want to take my badge?"

"I'd never ask you to do something that would put your job at risk." Nikki crossed her arms as she smiled at him. "It's not a big deal, really. I would have asked Quinn about it, but he had to rush off so fast. It's just a hunch I'm following up on."

"You know, if you let us do our jobs, we might actually solve this, without any help." Jim raised his eyebrows. "It's like we went to school for it or something."

"Two heads are always better than one." Nikki raised an eyebrow. "Didn't they teach you that in school?"

"I must have slept through that one." Jim cleared his throat, then grinned. "All right, what do you need?"

"I overheard a name that I'm curious about. I guess it's some kind of street name. The police maintain a sort of database of that kind of thing, right? Aliases, and who they belong to?" Nikki leaned back against the wall. "Do you think you could look up the name for me, and let me know what you find?"

"That sounds pretty harmless." Jim nodded. "Follow me." He led her through a maze of desks, to one in the back corner of the room. "Welcome to my humble abode." He smiled as he dropped down into the chair behind the desk. "It's not as fancy as Quinn's corner office, but it works for now."

"I think it's nice." Nikki noticed a stack of books on the corner of his desk. All were true crime novels. "I see you have a bit of an obsession?"

"Eh, when I have downtime, I like to do my research." Jim gave the books a light slap. "It's not often we get so much crime here in Dahlia, so I have to do something to keep my mind occupied."

"I can understand that." Nikki stood beside him as he typed on his computer.

"All logged in, so what's the name?" Jim glanced over at her, then scooted his chair a little to the side as he realized how close they were.

Nikki hid a smile. She guessed that he didn't want any trouble with Quinn.

"Wolf." Nikki frowned. "That's all I know. Is that enough?"

"Wolf. I haven't heard that one before. Let's see what comes up." Jim typed the name in, then suddenly stood up from his chair. "On second thought, this is probably not a good idea."

"What? Why not?" Nikki tried to peer past him at the screen.

"Don't." Jim glared at her. "Don't tell Quinn I

looked up the name for you, and don't keep looking into Wolf. Got it?"

"Jim, please, I just wanted some information, it's not like I'm going to hunt the guy down."

Jim straightened his shoulders. "I'll tell you what. You give Quinn a call and you ask him to look Wolf up." He crossed his arms. "I'm sorry, I can't help you."

Nikki stared at him in disbelief. She was tempted to push him out of the way and have a look but assaulting a police officer might be frowned upon in the middle of a police station.

"Fine, I will call Quinn."

"You do that." Jim continued to block the monitor.

"Thanks for your help." Nikki flashed him a warm smile, then hurried out of the station. She didn't feel in the clear until she made it out the front door. As soon as she did, she sighed. All she had was a call record, that might prove to lead to nothing. But she also knew that Jim had found something when he looked up the name Wolf, something so dangerous that he was unwilling to share it with her. The problem was, without the slightest bit of information she had no way to find out more or hunt him down.

When Nikki made it back to her apartment, she printed the pictures off her phone and sat down at the table with them and a highlighter. Sorting through the calls was a good distraction from her desire to find out just what Jim was hiding from her about Wolf.

CHAPTER 15

Sonia looked up from her cup of tea as she heard a light knock on the door.

"Come in, Nikki." She stood up, gave Nikki a quick hug and walked into the kitchen to pour another cup of tea. After receiving Nikki's text, she knew that it would only be a matter of time before she arrived.

"Hi Baby." Nikki crouched down to greet Princess. She gave her a kiss and a scratch behind the ear, then turned to Sonia. "I had to come see you to try and work this out. I think I'm going to burst if I don't find out who this Wolf person is. And, two heads are better than one."

"One step at a time." Sonia set her cup of tea down on the table. "We know that he's a dangerous guy, and from what you heard of the conversation with Betty, it's pretty clear that she's up to something."

"But what?" Nikki sat down across from her. "I got a copy of the call records to and from Marlo's shop the morning he was killed." She set the piece of paper down in the middle of the table.

"How?" Sonia looked up at her, her eyes wide. "Did Quinn give this to you?"

"Gave it to me or left it on his desk. I took some pictures of it." Nikki grinned. "Either way I got it."

"I see that." Sonia smiled a little. "All right, let's have a look."

"I think it's a complete record, but only some of the numbers have addresses connected to them. It looked like it was quite a busy morning with forty incoming calls, and five outgoing. I've highlighted fifteen minutes before and after our window of time of death until the time I arrived at the shop. But we really need to look into all the calls that morning, in case someone called earlier in the day to try to find out when he would be alone."

"Let's see, I'm guessing some of the incoming and outgoing calls had to be related to Pam's daughter, right?" Sonia looked over the list. "Yes, here." She pointed to one of the calls. "That's from the daycare, and this outgoing one after it is to Ethel's number."

"There are two calls to Ethel, it looks like she was really trying to get a hold of her." Nikki frowned. "I wonder what would have happened if Ethel had decided to go in."

"The fact that she didn't, points to the idea that she wanted to make sure that Marlo was alone. Now that I've seen Ethel in Philip's shop, it is possible that she made sure that Marlo would be alone for Philip's sake."

"Yes, it is." Nikki made a note on her phone. "But we also should consider that no one knew he would be alone. Someone might have walked in and just took the opportunity."

"Let's say, someone was watching the shop." Sonia's eyes widened as she looked up at Nikki. "Maybe this person saw Scott leave to make the deliveries, and then saw Pam leave to pick up her daughter. This person would have known that Marlo was alone."

"But not how long he would be alone." Nikki frowned. "Unless the person knew about Scott's deliveries, and knew that Pam was on her way to pick up her daughter. Didn't she mention something about not being able to reach her sitter to pick up her daughter?" She tapped her chin as she tried to recall. "I think she did. So, the sitter might be one more person that knew that Marlo would be alone. We should find out who the sitter is, and find out why she couldn't be reached, and if she's connected with any of our suspects besides Pam."

"I bet this is her number." Sonia pointed out a number called repeatedly between the calls to Ethel. "I'll give it a try."

"You do that, I'm going to keep looking for Wolf." Nikki typed on her phone while Sonia walked to the other side of the room to make the call.

Sonia scooped up Princess and held her in one arm and the phone in the other. She paced as she waited for the babysitter to answer the phone.

"Hello, how can I help you?" A sweet, young voice answered.

"Hi, I'm calling to ask you a few questions about the babysitting services you offer." Sonia held her breath as she wondered if she would believe her.

"Oh, right now I don't have any openings. But if you'd like me to put your name on a waiting list, I can. You can check out my website, it's Brianna's Playhouse, I update it when I have openings. What hours are you looking for?" The woman paused.

"What hours are you available?" Sonia looked at Nikki. She had no idea how to arrange daycare for a child. She hadn't had any of her own, and neither had Nikki. She hoped she could fudge her way through it.

"Until eight in the morning, and after three in the afternoon. I work at the Dahlia Hotel during the day. Do you have a school-aged child?" Brianna's voice lifted a little, as if Sonia's response left her a little suspicious.

"I'm looking for some information actually. I don't actually have a child for you to babysit." Sonia winced as she heard Brianna's sharp breath.

"So, this is some kind of scam?" Brianna sighed. "I really don't have time for this."

"Brianna please, wait. It's not a scam." Sonia frowned.

"No, I won't wait. I don't know what you're up to, but I don't want to have anything to do with it. Please, lose my number." Brianna ended the call.

"Well, that didn't go well." Sonia rolled her eyes as she set her phone down on the table. "At least I found out why Brianna couldn't pick up Pam's daughter from daycare. She's only available certain times. She has a day job at the Dahlia Hotel."

Nikki leaned back in her chair.

"It's actually a little disappointing that that's the case. I had hoped that we would get some kind of lead out of this."

"We still might." Sonia stood up from the table. "I have to go back to the hotel soon. There are some final decisions to make. I can't let this party get away from me, not after so many people have invested so much time and work into it. Maybe I can speak with Brianna again there."

"Hopefully. Is there anything I can help you with?" Nikki stood up from her chair.

"Not at the moment, I don't think. I just need to run over and sign some paperwork." Sonia walked with Nikki to the door. "I can't tell you how much I appreciated your help at the hotel yesterday."

"I didn't do much." Nikki shrugged.

"Just being there was plenty." Sonia hugged her.

"While you're there, can you check if Dale Winter is working? I really want to speak to him. While you were on the phone, I matched his number to a call that came in a few minutes before Marlo was killed. If Marlo answered, then Dale might have found out that he was in the butcher shop alone. He could have relayed that information to someone. Or maybe he heard something in the background that could lead to Marlo's killer."

Nikki sighed. "It might be something, but I doubt it."

"I'll let you know." Sonia nodded.

Sonia arrived at the hotel, uncertain whether Brianna would be willing to speak to her. It was a big hotel and she wasn't sure what area Brianna worked in. She walked up to the front desk and smiled at the man behind it.

"Hi Earl."

"Sonia, so good to see you." Earl smiled at her. "I trust everything is coming along well for the party?"

"Yes, just fine." Sonia leaned against the desk. "Could you tell me if Brianna is working today?"

"Uh, sure." Earl tapped a few keys on the keyboard in front of him, then looked up at the monitor. "Yes, she is. She's on the third floor at the moment. Did you need her for something?"

"Oh, nothing important, I'll find her myself." Sonia started to step away from the desk, then recalled Nikki's request. "Could you tell me if Dale is working?"

"Sure." Earl grinned. "You're not going to ask about all of the staff, are you?"

"No, this is the last one, I promise." Sonia smiled as she watched his fingers fly across the keys.

"Nope, not today. He has the day off." Earl looked up at her. "Anything else?"

"No, that's it. Thank you." Sonia stepped away from the desk, then she froze. She turned back to Earl.

"See, I knew you'd be back." Earl laughed as he hovered his hands over the keys. "Who am I looking up now?"

"Actually, I was wondering, can you tell me what Dale's schedule was this week?" Sonia raised an eyebrow.

"Let's see." Earl hit a few keys, then studied the monitor. "It looks like he was on all afternoons all week, until yesterday, when he was on morning shift. Any other questions?" He wiggled his fingers.

"No, that's it. For real this time." Sonia laughed and walked off towards the elevator. As she rode up to the third floor, she sent a text to Nikki with the information, as well as the fact that Dale hadn't been working on the morning of Marlo's murder.

As Sonia stepped out onto the third floor, she noticed the quiet that surrounded her. She also spotted a maid's cart about halfway down the hall. She tucked her phone into her purse and wondered just how she was going to convince Brianna to talk to her. She might be able to clear Pam as a suspect, or at the very least, give her some inside information about Pam's relationship with Marlo and Scott. She decided she would ask about Dale first.

Sonia waited near the cart and hoped that Brianna wouldn't recognize her voice. When one of the room doors opened, she smiled at the woman who stepped out.

"Brianna?"

"Do I know you?" Brianna stared at her for a long moment.

"We've probably met at some point before, I've been to this hotel many times." Sonia smiled. "Could you spare a minute to talk to me?"

"Not really, I am very busy. But if you walk with me, we can talk." Brianna pushed the cart down to the next room. "What is it about?"

"Dale Winter." Sonia watched Brianna's face tense in reaction to the name. "You know him, don't you?"

"Sure, everyone knows Dale." Brianna shrugged.

"He seems like such a nice guy." Sonia prodded, as she sensed that Brianna might disagree.

"Yes, he looks all sweet and calm, doesn't he?"

Brianna picked up a small stack of towels and walked towards the nearest door.

"What do you mean by that?" Sonia grabbed a stack of towels, then followed after her.

"What I mean is, it's the sweet ones that have the most to hide. I've been working here for a while, and Dale has, too. He's never done a single thing strange, never so much as raised his voice. But the other day, he lost it on a delivery driver. I have never seen him behave that way before. It was like he had turned into his father, so angry." Brianna popped open the door to the hotel room, then walked in with the stack of towels.

"A delivery driver? Was there a problem with the delivery?" Sonia followed after Brianna.

"No, there wasn't even supposed to be a delivery. That's the strange thing. The delivery had come the day before. I have no idea why he was going after that guy so harshly, but he looked like he wanted to grab him by the neck." Brianna turned around and nearly bumped into Sonia. "Oh, thank you." She smiled as she took the towels from her.

"Do you know who the driver was?" Sonia narrowed her eyes.

"It was the meat guy. The hotel gets a lot of deliveries, and I don't pay that much attention to who brings them, but I noticed this one because of the argument." Brianna led the way out of the hotel room.

"You said that it wasn't a day for a delivery? What day was it?" Sonia stepped in front of her cart, before she could push it any farther down the hall.

"Sometime last week." Brianna shrugged. "I don't know exactly."

"Not yesterday, or the day before?" Sonia tried to meet her eyes, but she was too busy counting the remaining towels on her cart.

"No, definitely not yesterday or the day before. I think it was almost a week ago, it could have even been a little longer." Brianna sighed as she looked down the hall. "Do you mind? I really have a lot of work to get done."

"Of course, just one more question, please?" Sonia walked alongside the cart as Brianna rolled it down the hallway.

"One more." Brianna nodded and stopped at another door.

"Do you remember anything about the conversation they had? Even just a few words or a phrase that might give you an idea of what the problem was?" Sonia looked into her eyes.

"Uh, it was a while ago." Brianna shook her head, then frowned. "I guess there was one thing. Like I said, it wasn't a delivery day, and I thought that I heard the delivery driver asking for something back. It didn't make any sense to me at the time."

"What do you think he was asking for back?" Sonia lowered her voice. "Did they mention anything specific?"

"Not really. But the driver kept saying that he needed it back, and that it was a mistake. That's all I know. Okay? Now, please. I do still have a job to do."

Sonia smiled. "Yes, I understand. Thank you for your help, I really appreciate it."

"Anything I can do to help." Brianna smiled, then stepped into a hotel room.

Sonia turned and walked back down the hallway. She still had the paperwork to finish, but she also had an update to send to Nikki. If her suspicions were right, Dale had an argument with Scott. That at least might lead to something. Now she knew that Dale was off on the morning of Marlo's murder, and he also had a problem with Scott. Could he have killed Marlo and mowed down Scott? She shook her head.

It makes no sense. He has no motive. Sonia

snapped her fingers. Unless there was more to that argument than just a delivery mix-up. After she rode the elevator back to the lobby, she pulled out her phone and called Nikki.

"Sonia, what did you find?"

"Something. I'm not sure what yet. But according to Brianna, Dale and a delivery driver, I'm guessing it was Scott, had an argument. Scott was demanding a delivery back, and Dale refused to give it to him. It seems like there might be something there." Sonia frowned. "I just can't put my finger on it."

"I'll see what I can find out. I'm going to see him now."

"I'll be finished here soon. Why don't you wait for me?" Sonia asked.

"No, that's okay. I just want to speak to him."

"Be careful, Nikki."

CHAPTER 16

*N*ikki took a deep breath, then walked up to Dale's front door. With Coco securely by her side, she knocked on the door. Maybe she wouldn't find out anything new, but he was the only person that she knew had argued with Scott before he was killed. She wanted to know what exactly they were arguing about, and as far as she knew he was the only source she could get that information from. With her mind focused on exactly what she would say to him when he opened the door, she hadn't considered what she would do if he didn't.

After several seconds passed, she knocked again. She'd seen him go into the house. She knew that he was inside. The question was, why wasn't he answering the door? Was he busy doing something else? Or had he peeked through the window and decided that he didn't want to speak with her? Maybe he thought she was some kind of salesperson.

"Dale?" Nikki called out through the front door. "Dale, are you in there?" She knocked again. At least if he knew that she knew his name, he might become curious enough to open the door.

Nikki held her breath as the knob began to turn. Once more she rehearsed the questions she had planned. Maybe she could coax him into telling the truth, maybe she could push him into revealing something that would open up the entire case.

"What do you want?" Dale spoke through a slight crack in the door.

"Dale, I just wanted to talk to you. I'm a friend of your father's." Nikki smiled at him as she waited for him to open the door.

The door didn't budge. "What do you want?"

"I was just wondering about a wrong delivery to the Dahlia Hotel? It was from Marlo's Butcher Shoppe. I guess Scott had tried to take it back, but you refused, why is that?"

"I don't know anything about any of that." Dale shook his head.

"Do you mind if I come in for a second?" Nikki tried to wedge her foot in the door.

"No, you can't come in." Dale glared at her through the small opening. "You're a liar."

"I'm not." Nikki forced a smile to her lips as she wondered why Dale was so suspicious of her. "I met your father at the hotel, he was helping my friend Sonia. You know Sonia Whitter, don't you?"

"I know Sonia, and I know who you are, and who your boyfriend is. I know that my father would never be friendly with someone who was so involved with the inept and corrupt police department that is ruining this town."

"What?" Nikki blinked as she heard the shift in his tone. He wasn't just suspicious, he was angry. And he wasn't going to back down about it. "I think there's been some kind of misunderstanding. Please, just open the door and we can talk about it. Will you just let me speak to you for a moment?"

Nikki took a slight step back as the door started to open farther. Just when she thought he would step out, he glared at her through the gap in the door.

"Who sent you?"

"Who sent me?" Nikki stared at him. "No one, Dale, no one sent me. I just wanted to speak with you. This is Coco." She smiled as she reached down to give the dog a light pat. "Don't worry, he's very friendly."

"Whoever sent you, you tell them that I have plenty of weapons in this house, and no one is going to take me out of here without a fight." Dale slammed the door shut.

Nikki's hand trembled as she pulled out her phone. She dialed Quinn's number as her heart pounded against her chest. If she didn't get help, she had no idea what Dale might do. It sounded to her as if he might have lost his mind.

"Nikki, where are you?" Quinn's tone sounded stern. "You didn't go after Wolf, did you?"

"I'm at Dale Winter's house." Nikki frowned. "Quinn, I think you need to get out here, with some backup."

"Nikki, what did you do?" Quinn's voice grew even more tense.

"I'm not sure. But something set him off. He says he has weapons in the house, but I'm not sure if he's telling the truth." Nikki took a step back from the front door.

"Nikki, are you safe?" Quinn's voice grew breathless.

"Yes." Nikki hurried down the driveway. "Yes, I think so. But I'm not so sure about anyone else."

"Get away from the house, we'll be there in a few minutes." Quinn ended the call.

Nikki shuddered as her mind struggled to process what she'd just discovered. Had Dale just confessed? Had he indicated that he was guilty, and he wasn't going to jail?

Nikki was still sorting through her thoughts when Quinn's car screeched up to the sidewalk, followed by several police cars.

Quinn jumped out of the car and ran up to her.

"Nikki, what are you still doing here?"

"I couldn't leave." Nikki bit into her bottom lip. "What if someone walked up to the house?"

"Nikki, you have to get to safety!" Quinn demanded.

"I just came here to talk to him, Quinn, I swear." Nikki looked into his eyes. "I had no idea he was going to do something like this."

"I understand, I believe you." Quinn placed his hands on her shoulders. "But I need you to stand clear, far back from the house. We're going to have to handle this now."

"But maybe if I could talk to him?" Nikki

frowned. "I'm just not sure what I said or did that set him off."

"In these situations, there's not always an explanation. Sometimes people just lose it. Dale has been on our radar because of some threats he's made around town. While we questioned others about Marlo and Scott's murders, his name came up more than once. Then we looked into some of his social media posts and found a pattern. We believe he may be a vigilante."

"A vigilante?" Nikki recalled the conversation that she'd overheard between John and Gus. John's words made more sense now. "Maybe he learned it from his father?"

"Wherever he learned it from, it's pretty clear that he's involved in this crime now. Which means he's going to feel as if he has nothing to lose. You're going to leave this to me." Quinn stared hard into her eyes. "Do you hear me?"

"Yes Quinn, I hear you." Nikki took a step back from him, and then continued until she and Coco made it across the street to the opposite sidewalk. As she stood there and watched the police surround Dale's house, she tried to imagine what it would be like to be him in that moment. Had he taken justice into his own hands and decided to kill Marlo? But why?

Nikki paced back and forth outside of the interrogation room. She couldn't hear a single thing that was said inside, but she could guess that Quinn was determined to get to the truth. As she waited for him to step out, she noticed a few of the police officers look in her direction. None asked her to leave, or even sit down.

"Coffee?" Jim held out a cup to her. "I thought maybe you could use some."

"Thank you." Nikki smiled at him as she took the cup. "This is just what I need, actually. They've been in there for so long."

"I'm sure he'll be done soon." Jim glanced at the door. "Hopefully, it'll lead to the murders being solved and we'll get our Christmas miracle."

"I hope so." Nikki smiled at the thought, then she took a sip of her coffee. She'd been piecing things together in her mind ever since Dale closed the door to his house on her. Why was Dale so angry? Nathan felt as if something was sketchy about Marlo's business. Did Dale know about what was going on there? Was Dale involved in it?

The door opened in front of Nikki and caused her to jump.

"Nikki." Quinn closed the door behind him. "Have you been out here the whole time?"

"What happened?" Nikki looked into his eyes.

"Over here." Quinn caught her by the arm and steered her down a short hallway that led to the stairwell. "I had hoped you would go home."

"Once I dropped Coco off, I came here. I need to know what happened, Quinn. Is Dale the murderer?" Nikki frowned.

"He's confessed to murdering Marlo. He hasn't gone into detail, yet. I am still trying to get him to tell me everything. But according to him, he overheard Nathan, the manager of Chop Chop, complaining about some suspicious activity that was happening at Marlo's shop. So, he began to stake it out to see what was happening. He had been watching the shop for over two weeks. He claims he saw a few of the same men approach the shop many times, always after hours. He recognized some of them as workers from some of the bars in Dahlia and surrounding towns. He suspected that the guys hanging around the shop and working at the bars were likely dealing drugs, and he couldn't stand the thought of the town being overrun with them."

"What about Wolf? Is he a dealer?"

"How did you know about Wolf?" Quinn asked. "I didn't tell you about him because I didn't want you investigating him."

"I think Betty is involved in this. She was on the phone to someone and he mentioned Wolf." Nikki grimaced.

"She was?" Quinn's eyes widened.

Nikki explained about how she heard Wolf's name.

"Wolf is involved in lots of illegal activity." Quinn nodded. "But the police have never been able to make anything stick."

"Tell me what Dale said about Marlo. Did Dale really just kill Marlo because he suspected he was dealing drugs?"

"He sent threatening letters to Marlo to try and get him to stop dealing. He wanted to clean up the streets of criminals. He said he saw, and called to confirm, that the shop was empty, and then he went inside to confront Marlo about the drug dealing. Marlo insisted he had no idea what he was talking about, and Dale lost his temper and killed him."

Quinn sighed. "I wish there was more of an explanation than that, but that is all he said."

"What about Scott?" Nikki searched his eyes. "Why did he kill Scott?"

"He insists that he didn't. It's still possible it was a random hit-and-run, but I'm going to work on Dale some more. My guess is that he thought Scott knew about the murder, so he decided he had to kill Scott, too. But that doesn't fit in with his white knight fantasies, so he's denying it."

"Sonia said that Brianna, an employee at Dahlia Hotel, said that the meat delivery guy and Dale had an argument a week or two ago about Dale not returning goods to him. I think it must have been Scott." Nikki shook her head. "Maybe it has something to do with the murder? Maybe you can ask Dale about it?"

"I will." Quinn wrapped his arms around her. "Now, will you please go home? I need you to be safe. All right? I need to know that you are somewhere safe."

"Maybe not home. Maybe, to Sonia's?" Nikki raised an eyebrow. "She's going to want to know about all of this."

"Of course." Quinn nodded, then glanced over

his shoulder at the door. "I'm going to let him stew a bit, then I'm going to question him again."

"Do you think he's right? Do you think that Marlo was really dealing drugs?" Nikki slipped her hands into her pockets. "How did none of us see it happening? How did he get away with it?"

"I don't know, yet. I don't have any evidence that points directly to drug dealing. There's certainly money that needs to be explained, and some individuals with bad reputations that were spotted coming and going from the shop on occasion, but at this point I haven't been able to completely connect the dots. What I do know is that Dale killed Marlo, and I believe he killed Scott too, to protect himself. But it's going to take us some time to get to that confession, I think. Tell Sonia I say to keep you safe. Christmas is almost here, and I don't want your parents to think that I let any harm come to you." Quinn caressed her cheek. "Please, I really want to make a good impression."

"You worry too much." Nikki kissed him lightly on the lips. "You're an amazing catch, and trust me, they'll see that."

"I'm a catch, huh?" Quinn grinned as he searched her eyes. "I'll have to remember that."

"You should." Nikki winked at him, then turned

to leave the police station. Dale had confessed to one murder, but not the other. Until he did, that left her wondering if there was a possibility that Scott had been killed by someone else. Perhaps by Wolf? But why? Had he been involved in the drug dealing himself? Overwhelmed, and exhausted, she headed for Sonia's house. A little time with Princess and Sonia would certainly help her to calm down and get her head straight.

CHAPTER 17

*W*hen Nikki knocked on Sonia's front door, Sonia opened it right away. Princess ran over to the door, tail wagging eagerly.

"Nikki, I was so worried!" She hugged her friend. "I've been watching the news, and I knew, I just knew that you were involved. I was trying to reach you."

"I'm okay. I'm sorry, I had my phone on silent." Nikki hugged her back then crouched down to pet Princess. She picked her up and cuddled her. "Dale didn't do anything to hurt me. But he has confessed to Marlo's murder."

"Oh, thank goodness." Sonia pressed her hand against her chest. "Finally, we have some answers.

What a relief that is." She looked into Nikki's eyes. "It is a relief, isn't it?"

"It is." Nikki sighed.

Nikki explained what happened with Dale in detail as she ran her hand over Princess' head.

"Wow, that must have been scary."

"It was." Nikki nodded.

"At least it's all over now." Sonia and Nikki walked over to the couch and sat down. "Now, you can focus on getting ready for the holidays."

"I know. Only three days to go." Nikki's heart raced again at the thought of meeting Quinn's parents. At least the murder was solved so she could concentrate on taking care of the dogs and getting ready for the holidays.

"I have an appointment with the singers for the party soon." Sonia smiled. "Would you like to come with me, or I can cancel it, if you want me to spend time with you."

"No, that's okay, I need to do the walks, anyway." Nikki stood up and walked with her to the door. "Do you want me to take Princess as well."

"No, thanks. She's already had a walk and I am going to take her with me, she loves listening to Christmas carols."

"Oh, that sounds like fun." Nikki smiled.

"It is. Sometimes she howls along with them." Sonia picked up Princess and gave her a cuddle.

"Cute. Call me if you need anything." Nikki hugged Sonia, gave Princess a kiss on the head, then stepped out the door.

As Nikki took a breath of the fresh air, she smiled to herself. Yes, she knew exactly what she needed to do. She needed to walk Rocky and Bruno, the one thing she was sure would help her relax. It was a little early for their walk, but she didn't think the dogs would mind. She ducked back to her apartment to grab her supplies, then headed out.

As Nikki picked up the dogs, she felt a little calmer. Being surrounded by Rocky and Bruno gave her an instant feeling of happiness.

Christmas music played through the speakers mounted outside one of the shops on the main street. It put a bit of a skip in her step. Yes, things had been rough, but now she could look forward to Christmas. With only three days left to prepare, she knew that she would have to work hard to get everything done, but it would be worth it.

Nikki glanced through the window of one of the

shops and admired a train that chugged around the Christmas tree on display. She began to relax. As she neared Marlo's shop, she noticed that the neon sign was off. Perhaps Carolyn had finally filled the orders and could take a break. She considered the possibility of inviting her to Christmas dinner. With her thoughts still focused on the festivities ahead, she didn't notice Rocky's low growl at first.

When Bruno followed it up with a sharp bark and tug at the end of his leash, she snapped to attention.

"It's all right boys, settle down." Nikki shortened their leashes.

Rocky and Bruno lunged towards Marlo's shop, and then the parking lot beside it. Curious, Nikki decided to let the dogs lead the way. Maybe they had discovered a squirrel or a stray cat.

The dogs led her around the corner of the building, to the small lot behind it, where the delivery van was parked. Nikki noticed a light on inside the shop. Maybe someone had forgotten to turn it off? The dogs pulled harder towards the back of the van.

Nikki struggled to keep them under control.

"Enough!" She frowned as she stared down at Rocky and Bruno. "I don't know what your life was like before you came here, but things are different now. We can't just hunt down random things or people."

Bruno dug his paws against the pavement and lowered his head. He pulled as hard as he could on the leash, which caused Nikki to stumble forward a few steps. As she did, she caught sight of the back doors of the van. They hung wide open. She tied the dogs up to a pole on the side of the lot. She didn't want them to get into trouble. Nikki peered inside the van, curious as to what the dogs might be barking at. She saw only a few rolling shelves with empty boxes on them. As she leaned in a little closer, she noticed that there were little pouches of a white colored substance lining the red boxes. If there had been meat on top, they would have been completely hidden. Her heart began to race as she realized what they were. If Marlo was dead, and Scott was dead, who had loaded the boxes with drugs?

Nikki heard a clatter behind her and spun around in time to see Carolyn with stacks of wrapped meat in her hands.

"You!" Nikki gasped.

"Great, just great." Carolyn shoved Nikki hard into the back of the van.

Nikki tried to keep her footing, but the backs of

her knees struck the end of the van, and she buckled. Carolyn grabbed her legs and flung them into the van, sending Nikki off balance as she tried to sit up. Her cheek struck the side of the van. A burst of pain carried through her senses, deafened only by the slam of the van doors. She heard something slide into place. She rushed to the doors and pushed as hard as she could, but they wouldn't budge.

The van engine turned on, and then the van lurched forward. Nikki's heart pounded as she realized she had just been abducted by at the very least a drug dealer, and likely a killer as well. She braced herself against the side of the van and tried to think of a way out. She was aware that the van was refrigerated, but she couldn't think about how cold it was, she had to try to survive. As the van rumbled on, she realized that her only option was getting through the back doors. If she could get them to open, she could roll to safety.

Nikki kicked the rear doors of the van as hard as she could. Her legs ached from the repeated kicking. But no matter how hard she tried, she couldn't get them to pop open. As her body jostled around in the van, she could feel the change from the highway, to a less smooth road. Her stomach churned as she wondered where Carolyn intended to take her. There was no doubt in her mind that she wouldn't leave her alive. Now that she knew that Carolyn had been dealing drugs, had she been the one to kill Marlo, and Scott? Was she in on it with her brother? Did he double cross her and she killed him? Or did they get into a disagreement over it? Had Marlo found out what she was doing and confronted her about it, so she killed him? Had Scott witnessed it, so she killed him to keep him quiet? But then why had Dale confessed to killing Marlo?

Nikki pinned her feet against the rear doors to keep herself steady and looked around for anything that she could use to protect herself. Other than the rolling shelves and boxes, there wasn't anything else in the back of the van. The shelves were locked into place at the moment, and she had no idea how to release them.

Nikki's thoughts traveled to the dogs. She had heard them barking at the van as it pulled away. It gave her some comfort to think that Carolyn hadn't harmed the dogs, but she hoped that they would be okay. No one would have any idea where she had gone. No one would know to look for her at Marlo's shop and certainly no one knew that she had been peering into the back of one of Marlo's delivery vans when she disappeared. She'd heard the crunch of her phone when Carolyn smashed it. She doubted it would be of any use. She was alone, and she had to find a way to survive.

CHAPTER 18

*T*he van lurched to a stop, and the engine turned off.

Nikki squeezed her eyes shut. She pulled her feet back a few inches from the doors and waited for Carolyn to open them. If she could at least get a swift kick in, then she might get the upper hand.

Carolyn knocked sharply on the doors. "Don't try anything stupid in there."

Nikki bit into her bottom lip. She stared hard at the doors. The moment they popped open, she slammed her feet forward. Instead of hitting Carolyn, she hit the steel doors, hard. Carolyn had swung them back in a second after she opened them and struck Nikki's feet hard.

Nikki cried out, as pain burst through her ankles and shins.

"I said, don't do anything stupid." Carolyn frowned as she swung the doors open again. This time she pointed a gun at Nikki. "Let's go, out of the van."

"Carolyn, please." Nikki stared into her eyes. "You don't have to do this. You can just let me go."

"Right, so you can run to your detective boyfriend?" Carolyn shook her head. "No, sorry. That would be very bad for business. Let's just get this over with. I have more deliveries to make."

Nikki shuddered with fear and drew her knees up to her chest.

"No!"

"No?" Carolyn pointed the gun straight at Nikki. "No, is not an option."

Nikki's heart pounded. She didn't doubt that Carolyn would pull the trigger. She'd killed before, she was certain that she would kill again.

"Is this what you did to Marlo? When he found out about you being involved with dealing drugs?"

"Marlo?" Carolyn narrowed her eyes. "I didn't hurt Marlo. I would never have hurt my brother."

"Because he always tried to protect you." Nikki took a slow breath. She knew that she had to keep her wits about her, it was the only chance she had of getting out of this alive. "Did he even know about the drugs?"

"Marlo didn't want to face the truth. When I showed up, his finances were a mess, his business was about to fold, he was going to lose everything, even his apartment, but instead of taking my advice, he hatched his own stupid plan. He was going to put some roaches in Chop Chop's food and then make false reviews and postings, hoping the Health Department would get involved. Just like he had done to Philip. I warned him they would put two and two together, and not only would he not succeed in destroying Chop Chop's business, he would likely lose his right to operate his own, if not go to jail." She rolled her eyes. "Of course, he wouldn't listen to a word I said. So, I had to take matters into my own hands. Betty and Scott helped me. They needed a little extra cash. I organized it all. It's amazing what money buys. Not only did we get extra money from the meat sales to the bars and restaurants, but we also got the money from selling the drugs to them. The meat was the perfect cover to move the drugs to the workers that sold them. Now, the police found some of the money and I need to work extra hard to replace it. Marlo didn't even know about the money hidden in his apartment. If only I had time to move it, before the police got to it." She took a deep breath of the crisp air, then smiled as she shook her head. "It's funny, when you get involved with drug dealers, you get to know some deep, dark places. Places that most people probably don't even know exist." She pushed Nikki ahead of her. "Keep walking, we're almost there."

The farther Nikki walked down the hill, the more her knees threatened to buckle. A deep sense of dread settled into her stomach. Her entire body felt heavier than it ever had before. She wasn't going to get out of this alive, she had no idea how she could escape.

"Over there." Carolyn pushed her in the direction of an old, wooden bridge that stretched from one side of a large gap to the other.

"It wasn't Dale that killed Scott, was it?" Nikki suddenly whirled around to face her.

"It's Dale that will go to jail for it." Carolyn pointed her gun directly at Nikki. "It's what all of Dahlia will believe."

"Not all of Dahlia." Nikki narrowed her eyes. "They're already on to you. They know that you were distributing drugs to the bars and restaurants so that they could sell them."

"No, they know that my brother was. They know that he was killed for it, and that Scott was, too." Carolyn smiled, then shook her head. "They don't know anything about me."

"I do." Nikki took a sharp breath as she studied the woman's expression. "I know that it was you that killed Scott."

"What?" Carolyn pursed her lips. "Why would I do that? No one will believe it."

"You did it because you loved Marlo so much." Nikki bit into her bottom lip as a rush of empathy surfaced within her. Despite the fact that Carolyn pointed a gun at her, and intended to murder her, Nikki felt bad for her. "You did it because your brother, your family, the person who had always protected you, was murdered. You did it because you thought that Scott murdered him."

"Keep quiet." Carolyn tightened her grasp on the gun. "You don't know what you're talking about."

"Yes, I do." Nikki's heart raced as she saw the fear and grief in Carolyn's eyes. "You thought that Marlo found out about you and Scott. You thought that he had threatened to fire Scott or make him pay if he didn't stay away from you. You thought Scott murdered him because of it. When you realized that, you knew you couldn't let Scott live. You had to get revenge. The only person that ever really meant anything to you in life was gone, and someone needed to pay for that crime. So, you killed Scott, didn't you?"

"How was I supposed to know that some creepy vigilante would be watching my brother?" Carolyn frowned as she lowered the weapon slightly. "Not that it is a problem for me, now. At least I have someone to blame for Scott's death."

"Don't you feel any guilt for murdering him? He didn't do anything wrong." Nikki edged a few steps back.

"No, not at all. I did what I thought I had to do. That's what real life is, Nikki. Real life isn't this picturesque little town, and your happy little life. Real life demands that you make choices. I made a choice. I don't regret it." Carolyn raised the gun higher again. "I won't regret this either. In the end, all that matters is surviving, and I can't let you ruin my life."

"Think about this, Carolyn. You're not a killer, you were just surviving. I want to survive, too. I'll keep my mouth shut to keep myself safe, you know I will." Nikki's heart slammed against her chest.

"I'd believe that, if I was a fool. You don't have the heart for lying, Nikki. You would tell the truth, eventually." Carolyn shook her head then put her finger on the trigger. "Don't take it personally, it's just business."

A sudden flurry of barks caused Carolyn to spin around. Nikki took that moment to shove her hard to the ground. She pinned her down against the dirt.

The woman beneath her squirmed and struggled to get out from under her, while still clinging to her gun.

"Nikki!" Quinn shouted as he rushed down the hill in her direction.

Rocky and Bruno howled as they surged towards her.

Nikki used all of her strength to hold Carolyn down, but she sensed that the woman was far stronger as she bucked up against her. She began to panic as she wondered what Carolyn would do if she was able to get free. Would she shoot Quinn? She reached for the hand that held the gun.

"Stay down!" Quinn shouted from a few feet away. "Let go of the gun and stay down on the ground!"

"Just kill me!" Carolyn wailed as she threw Nikki off her back and got up on her knees. "I have nothing left!" She swung the gun in Quinn's direction.

"No!" Nikki shrieked as she struggled to get back on her feet. Before she could, Rocky jumped forward and sank his teeth into Carolyn's wrist. He pulled her hand to the ground as Bruno jumped on top of the woman's back and pinned her down to the ground.

"Easy boys, easy." Quinn kicked the gun away from Carolyn's hand.

Carolyn pressed her face against the ground as she wept.

"Nikki." Quinn looked over at her. "Are you okay? Are you hurt?"

"I'm fine." Nikki shivered as she gazed into his eyes. "How did you find me?"

"Release!" Quinn commanded the dogs, then pulled Carolyn's hands behind her back. Once she was handcuffed, he looked back at Nikki. "I ran into Petra and she said that her friend was doing fine after surgery, so she went to visit him. It turns out that they are retired border patrol dogs, trained to look for drugs. Once I realized that, I knew why they had attacked Scott and barked at the van. The drugs were hidden in the meat. Even though we didn't find any drugs in our searches the smell must have lingered. I confronted Dale with the information about the fact that I knew he had an argument with Scott and that drugs were in the van. He admitted that one day when Scott made a meat delivery to the hotel, he asked Dale to grab one of the green boxes out of the van. But Dale is colorblind."

"Like his father." Nikki snapped her fingers.

"Yes, I guess so. Anyway, he grabbed the wrong box by mistake. He claims when he looked under the meat, there were packages of cocaine." Quinn shook his head. "He says he destroyed the drugs, and then Scott came back, demanding that he return the box. He refused, and Scott threatened him. He didn't tell me at first because he knew it would make it look like he had murdered Scott. I went to check the van out and found that it wasn't there, but I did find the dogs." He smiled at them. "I traced your phone and found it smashed in the parking lot. I guessed that you were in the van. I tracked the van by its license plate and found where it turned off the highway. I knew it was headed in the direction of one of Wolf's known haunts. I borrowed Rocky and Bruno, and we came looking for you. They sniffed you out." He gazed at her as he gathered the dogs' leashes. "Nikki, I thought I'd lost you."

"I thought I'd lost you, too." Tears sprang to Nikki's eyes.

"Betty gave us a lead on Wolf, and it looks like we are finally going to be able to make something stick and put him behind bars." Quinn smiled.

"Well, it looks like this has led to many criminals being taken off the street." Nikki smiled slightly. "It wasn't Dale that killed Scott. It was Carolyn. She thought that Scott had killed Marlo, and she wanted revenge."

"We've got the murderers now." Quinn looked back at Carolyn as sirens blared in the distance. "It's all over now, Nikki." He pulled her into his arms and ran his hand down through her hair. "Finally."

$\mathcal{N}$ikki stared into the mirror. The only souvenir she had of the past few days was a faint bruise on her cheek from being pushed into the van. It seemed like nothing, compared to what she'd been through. She took a deep breath and willed herself not to be nervous as she smoothed down the skirt of her spaghetti strap, knee length, red dress. Was it too tight? Not dressy enough?

"We're here!" A sing-song voice called out from the front door.

Nikki's chest tightened. This was it. This was the moment that she would meet Quinn's mother, and she guessed, the moment that his mother would decide whether Nikki was worthy of her son or not.

She braced herself as she inched towards the living room.

Spots almost knocked her over as he barreled towards the door.

"Spots, no!" Nikki reached for his collar, but he bolted out of her reach, and jumped up against Quinn's mother's legs.

"Oh my!" Ana gasped and stumbled back into her husband's grasp. "Well, aren't you a rowdy beast."

"I'm so sorry." Nikki caught Spots by the collar and tugged him back away from Quinn's mother. "Mrs. Grant, this is Spots, he doesn't usually behave this way. It's just there's so much excitement."

"That's a dog that could use a good trainer." Quinn's father squinted at her. "Aren't you a dog trainer of some sort?"

"She's a dog walker, Dad." Quinn stepped out of the kitchen and spread his arms wide to his mother. "I'm so glad you made it, thanks for coming all this way."

"Of course." Ana hugged him tight. "Though it was a rough drive."

"The traffic." Quinn's father moaned.

"Can I take your coat, Mr. Grant?" Nikki held out her hand.

"Call me Lance. No don't bother, I can find a place for it." He cleared his throat. "I see you've kept the place in good shape." He walked past Nikki, farther into the living room. "Not bad, not bad."

"Thanks." Quinn grinned. "I had to do a few repairs on the roof, but nothing too serious."

"Glad to hear it." Lance smacked his stomach. "Now, when's dinner?"

"Oh, it should be here soon." Quinn glanced at his watch. "Nikki's family is due to arrive soon as well."

"Dinner should be here soon?" Ana sniffed the air. "Do you mean to tell me we came all this way and we're not getting a home-cooked meal?"

"Mom, it's been a busy time. I thought it might be best if we had it catered." Quinn glanced over at Nikki. "That way everyone gets to enjoy the meal, and no one is exhausted."

"Huh. That would have been nice when I was young." Ana fluffed her hair, then winked at Nikki. "All these things that modern women get away with. Sometimes I wonder if women can even boil an egg anymore."

"Mom." Quinn sighed.

"What?" Ana's eyes widened. "I just said I

wondered, it's not like I'm going to send her into the kitchen to prove it."

Nikki gulped as she wondered how she would survive this meal. Already she had a few strikes against her.

"Why don't you sit down, we'll bring you out some wine." Quinn wrapped his arm around Nikki's shoulders and steered her into the kitchen.

"Oh Quinn, this is terrible." Nikki turned to face him.

Quinn instantly swept her into a passionate kiss.

Nikki laughed as she stumbled back.

"What was that for?"

Quinn looked up at the mistletoe then back into her eyes.

"She's always cranky after a long drive. Just try to relax. I promise, she's not as wicked as she seems." Quinn held her gaze.

"I don't think she's wicked." Nikki blushed.

"Sure." Quinn grinned at her. "Let's get that wine."

Moments later there was another knock on the door. Nikki's heart pounded as she guessed it would be her own family. At least she knew what to expect with them. As Quinn delivered the wine to his parents, Nikki opened the door for hers.

"Nikki!" Both of her parents cried out her name at the same time, then threw their arms around her.

"Stop, she can't breathe!" Kyle laughed as he tugged them free. "Don't suffocate her before dinner."

"I've missed you, too." Nikki smiled at them both, then hugged Kyle. "And even you."

"I should hope so." Kyle ruffled her hair. "Where's the food?"

"It'll be here soon." Nikki led them inside.

"It'll be here soon?" Nikki's mother raised an eyebrow. "Did you order pizza?"

"That's exactly what I was thinking." Ana laughed from the couch. "Kids these days."

Nikki shied back and allowed Quinn to make the introductions, while Kyle and Spots wrestled on the floor together. Before she could close the door, Sonia poked her head inside with Princess in her arms.

"Am I late?" She smiled.

"You're just in time." Nikki hugged her and Princess tight. "I need a friendly face around here."

"You're surrounded by people who love you." Sonia gave her a light squeeze then gave Princess a kiss on the cheek and put her on the floor. She ran over to play with Spots and Kyle. "What a wonderful holiday."

"We didn't have a chance to talk this morning. How was the party, yesterday?" Nikki asked.

"Great. It went off without a hitch. Well, except for the fact that Princess wouldn't wear her new Santa hat." Sonia laughed. "We managed to raise a lot of money for charity."

"That's great." Nikki's voice rose with enthusiasm.

"Were you able to get everything done?" Sonia looked around the room.

"Yes, Quinn and I decided not to get presents for each other this year. Instead we'll donate some money to the shelter in Spots' name. They do such a good job. I got the dogs' presents last night." Nikki pointed to the Christmas tree. "Princess' present is under there. Nothing like a ball on a rope to make a dog's tail wag happily."

"Oh." Sonia laughed. "Too true. Sounds like fun."

"So, where exactly is the food?" Nikki's father rubbed his stomach as he walked up to Nikki. "I'm starving."

"I'm checking on it, now." Quinn pressed the

phone against his ear, then offered him a glass of wine. "Something to hold you over?"

"What's this?" Nikki's father sniffed the glass. "Oh, cheap wine on an empty stomach, this should be fun." He rolled his eyes then took a sip.

"I'm sorry, I didn't know if there was a particular kind you liked." Quinn held up one finger to indicate he would be a second, then turned away as he talked into the phone. "Yes, the delivery was supposed to be here twenty minutes ago."

"Are we at least eating off of real plates?" Ana called out. "I can help set the table."

Nikki took a deep breath. "I'm not sure I can do this," she whispered to Sonia.

"No?" Sonia looked into her eyes. "About a week ago, we didn't think having this celebration would even be possible. Just three days ago, you were held at gunpoint by a murderer." Sonia smiled. "I think you are underestimating what you can handle."

"That's a good point." Nikki managed a smile. "I am just so grateful that everyone is here, but it would be nice if things went a little more smoothly."

"Put on some music, get the dishes out, soon everyone will be getting along." Sonia gave her a light pat on the shoulder. "Trust me, I've done this a few times."

"Thanks Sonia." Nikki took another deep breath as she walked over to the sound system. She started up some Christmas carols, then lit the candles on the dining room table. As everyone pitched in to set the table, she began to relax. Sonia was right. A few days ago, she had believed that she might not be around to see Christmas. All of a sudden, it didn't matter if the food didn't show up. It didn't matter if the wine wasn't right, or if Ana might wonder if she could even cook a meal. All that mattered was that they were all together, and for that, she felt blessed.

"Everything okay?" Quinn caught her by the hand and pulled her gently away from the table. He searched her eyes. "I know this is stressful, I know that you wanted things to be perfect."

"They are perfect." Nikki gazed into his eyes. "I don't think they could be any more perfect." She kissed him, just as the doorbell rang.

Quinn laughed as he pulled away from her. "I'm glad you're in good spirits, but I think these people are going to try to eat us if we don't get the food on the table."

"The food has arrived!" Sonia sung out from the front door.

Nikki laughed at the mad rush towards the door. The delivery boy stumbled back as he held out the boxes and bags.

Soon, the table was covered with a feast. Aromas that Nikki couldn't begin to describe filled the air, and her family, as well as Quinn's family, circled the table. As Sonia raised her glass of wine to make a toast, Nikki took another deep breath. Yes, everything was perfect. Two murders had been solved, her life had been saved, and now she could raise her glass, to celebrate with all of the wonderful people in her life. She didn't think anything could be better than that, until, Spots put his head on her knee.

Nikki smiled to herself as she gave his head a light pat under the table. Yes, she was very blessed.

The End

ALSO BY CINDY BELL

WAGGING TAIL COZY MYSTERIES

Murder at Pawprint Creek (prequel)

Murder at Pooch Park

Murder at the Pet Boutique

A Merry Murder at St. Bernard Cabins

Murder at the Dog Training Academy

Murder at Corgi Country Club

DUNE HOUSE COZY MYSTERIES

Seaside Secrets

Boats and Bad Guys

Treasured History

Hidden Hideaways

Dodgy Dealings

Suspects and Surprises

Ruffled Feathers

A Fishy Discovery

Danger in the Depths

Celebrities and Chaos

Pups, Pilots and Peril

Tides, Trails and Trouble

Racing and Robberies

Athletes and Alibis

Manuscripts and Deadly Motives

Pelicans, Pier and Poison

Sand, Sea and a Skeleton

NUTS ABOUT NUTS COZY MYSTERIES

A Tough Case to Crack

A Seed of Doubt

Roasted Peanuts and Peril

Chestnuts, Camping and Culprits

CHOCOLATE CENTERED COZY MYSTERIES

The Sweet Smell of Murder

A Deadly Delicious Delivery

A Bitter Sweet Murder

A Treacherous Tasty Trail

Pastry and Peril

Trouble and Treats

Fudge Films and Felonies

Custom-Made Murder

Skydiving, Soufflés and Sabotage

Christmas Chocolates and Crimes

Hot Chocolate and Homicide

Chocolate Caramels and Conmen

Picnics, Pies and Lies

Devils Food Cake and Drama

Cinnamon and a Corspe

Cherries, Berries and a Body

DONUT TRUCK COZY MYSTERIES

Deadly Deals and Donuts

Fatal Festive Donuts

Bunny Donuts and a Body

Strawberry Donuts and Scandal

Frosted Donuts and Fatal Falls

SAGE GARDENS COZY MYSTERIES

Birthdays Can Be Deadly

Money Can Be Deadly

Trust Can Be Deadly

Ties Can Be Deadly

Rocks Can Be Deadly

Jewelry Can Be Deadly

Numbers Can Be Deadly

Memories Can Be Deadly

Paintings Can Be Deadly

Snow Can Be Deadly

Tea Can Be Deadly

Greed Can Be Deadly

Clutter Can Be Deadly

BEKKI THE BEAUTICIAN COZY MYSTERIES

Hairspray and Homicide

A Dyed Blonde and a Dead Body

Mascara and Murder

Pageant and Poison

Conditioner and a Corpse

Mistletoe, Makeup and Murder

Hairpin, Hair Dryer and Homicide

Blush, a Bride and a Body

Shampoo and a Stiff

Cosmetics, a Cruise and a Killer

Lipstick, a Long Iron and Lifeless

Camping, Concealer and Criminals

Treated and Dyed

A Wrinkle-Free Murder

A MACARON PATISSERIE COZY MYSTERY SERIES

Sifting for Suspects

Recipes and Revenge

Mansions, Macarons and Murder

HEAVENLY HIGHLAND INN COZY MYSTERIES

Murdering the Roses

Dead in the Daisies

Killing the Carnations

Drowning the Daffodils

ABOUT THE AUTHOR

Cindy Bell is a USA Today and Wall Street Journal Bestselling Author. She is the author of the cozy mystery series Wagging Tail, Donut Truck, Dune House, Sage Gardens, Chocolate Centered, Macaron Patisserie, Nuts about Nuts, Bekki the Beautician, Heavenly Highland Inn and Wendy the Wedding Planner.

Cindy has always loved reading, but it is only recently that she has discovered her passion for writing romantic cozy mysteries. She loves walking along the beach thinking of the next adventure her characters can embark on.

You can sign up for her newsletter so you are notified of her latest releases at http://www.cindybellbooks.com.